HAPPY HONEYPOTS

SWINGING IN HARMONY

RICHARD LEE

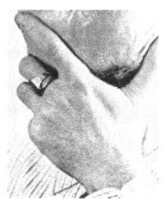

Dedicated to a world in need of
love and imagination.

"You only live once, but if you do it right, once is enough." - Mae West

FOREWORD

Charlotte and Henry Logan, and Harriet and George Jones, have been neighbours for many years. Their children grew up and went to university together, and they thought that their lives were quite normal. But then something happened.

PREFACE

"Well! I think we should try and open up our husbands to these ideas. We don't want them clamping up at the party. We know how men can hang on to fixed beliefs even when there is evidence of a benefit from change.

"I've got a plan that will change them, at least in part."

"And your plan is?"

"You and I are going to swap husbands for a night. We both know that this will lead to change of some sort. Hopefully, when we get to the party, George and Henry will fearlessly embrace the idea of swinging."

ONE

UNBUNDLING THE HUSBANDS

"Is that you Henry? I've left my glasses in my bag and you know I'm lost without them when I'm in a dark space. It doesn't feel like you but whoever it is, it does feel nice. If you're not Henry, perhaps you should tell me your name if you are intending to get intimate with me. Even if I cannot see you properly at least I'll know who I was with. And while I'm thinking about it, where are we going?"

There was silence, then a woman's voice close by answered.

"I think you've got my George, Lottie, and I'm pretty sure that what I've got in my hand belongs to your Henry. Is it okay if he knobs me darling? George will give you a good go, I'm sure. A couple of drinks and he usually wants it doggy style. And he'll go forever. Just thought you should know. I'm sure you will love it.

"Oh, and I think we're heading for the Pink Room, Lottie."

There was silence for a moment as Charlotte reviewed her situation.

"Well, Hetty. If we both enjoy today, I suppose it could be something we can do at home. Would you be up for it? Swapping our husbands on a Sunday afternoon could become something we could do instead of going for a drive."

"Indeed, Lottie! Being knobbed sounds much better than going to a plant nursery or art gallery. And if it works, we could ask our neighbours Doreen and Stacey if they were interested in doing it. I reckon both of their blokes could be good for something a little different.

So went the conversation Charlotte Logan and Harriet Jones had two weeks earlier. It was during a party they attended in a large house only a few blocks away from where they lived.

The official looking party invitation was beautifully printed on cream wove paper and adorned with hearts and cherubs.

'I take pleasure in inviting you to a party for adults only, at the address below. Anything goes, but don't feel you have to involve yourself in anything that does not appeal to you or goes against your moral judgement.

Signed, Ursula Lacey'

So what happened to the Logan and Jones couples in the lead up to this party and after they had received their invites?

Firstly, both women were unsure whether to mention it as neither could be certain that the other had received the same invite and if they hadn't it might be a little embarrassing for many reasons. To make things more complicated, Charlotte and Henry had been part of an event while they were away in their caravan mid-year which they had chosen not to speak of to anyone, even their neighbours, and that event might account for them receiving the invite even though they couldn't see how there could be a connection.

Harriet wasn't going to say anything either. Being a bit of a snob as well as what some would call a control freak, she thought that maybe she and George were on an exclusive mailing list of some sort and their friends across the road may not have been on that list.

George and Harriet were the owners of a large canvas goods business that George had inherited. He and Harriet were known to many of the well-heeled yacht owning families of the wealthy inner Sydney suburbs, and so receiving invitations was a common event.

Harriet ran her own bespoke curtain making business inside her husbands factory, utilising the machinery, the buying power and sometimes the available spare labour of his larger enterprise.

The Bespoke Curtain Company specialised in fulfilling the window covering market for large modern houses, grand house updates, blocks of new apartments and corporate offices and showrooms.

. . .

Both couples were well off in their own right. Henry Logan was a senior public servant and worked at the university. He involved himself in left-of-centre causes. Charlotte held a senior job at an inner-city welfare agency which, although it didn't pay a huge salary, gave her strong street credentials among their left-leaning friends.

Despite their social and political difference, these neighbours had been friends for many years. Both had children early and it was natural that their kids had grown up enjoying one another's company. Politics aside, the two couples agreed about almost everything and they liked each other very much.

If there was an obvious difference of any sort, it was the way each chose to spend their annual holidays. The Jones's closed their factory for a month in mid-winter and flew to London and Paris. The Logan's updated their medium-sized state-of-the-art caravan every three years, towing it north along the coast at around the same time that their neighbours flew overseas, and this is how things had been for a long time.

The two couples seemed happy with who they were. All four were aged around the mid forties although Harriet rightly claimed junior status.

Henry and Charlotte had met when they were twenty and twenty-one at a party following a protest march for something or other.

Henry was quite small and lithe and handsome and tanned, though prematurely grey. Charlotte wore the ageless angelic doll-like face of her youth and still wore her hair in a pony tail. She wore thick rimmed glasses. She was the same height as her husband. Her feet and hands were tiny but the rest of her body leant towards a slightly heavier dimension, most noticeably her buttocks. Her bottom, especially when she wore a tight fitting skirt, attracted attention from both men and women.

The couple were sweet and cheerful and loving and everyone adored them.

Harriet was the classic trophy wife of the successful business man. She and George met at university. Hetty could easily have been a fashion model. She was slim, long limbed and elegant. She knew about clothes and fashion and she was brilliant with figures. She was very good at estimating and calculating everything and she took pride in measuring-up each and every curtain job sent to her business – large or small – ensuring that there was never any wasted material or production time.

She and George were a successful partnership as well as a solid couple.

. . .

The problem of the invitations was solved for both women when Charlotte walked over to the Jones's the following Saturday morning with a large envelope containing an interior design magazine that had landed in the Logan's mail box by mistake.

"Hello! Is there anyone home?"

"Come in Lottie. I'm just brewing some coffee so well timed!"

Charlotte dropped the large envelope at the end of the bench where a pile of other mail sat waiting attention and adjusted her glasses.

"Oh! You've got one too."

An identical envelope to the one containing the Logan's party invite lay atop the pile of mail. Charlotte could see that it had been opened.

"We thought we'd go just for the hell of it. It could be awful but then it could be fun. From the little I know of Ursula, she seems very capable so I expect it will be well organised. What about you, Hetty? Will you and George be going?"

Harriet fixed Charlotte with that analytical stare she sometimes made when cautiously calculating a response.

"Yes, we talked about it and George said he was happy to go. I wasn't sure to begin with but then thought what the hell. And now I know you two are going, it makes it easier. We can hang out together and enjoy the party without feeling we are the odd ones out, if and when it gets raunchy."

Charlotte stared back at her friend, her angelic smile a defence against any possible rebuke.

"Who knows, Hetty, you and George might get raunchy yourselves. Letting ourselves go once in a while can't be too dangerous. Can it?"

Charlotte thought she noticed a slight moment of confusion or was it alarm, as Harriet formulated her reply.

"You surprise me, Lottie. You sound almost excited by the idea. Can I ask if you and Henry have travelled the swinging path before? Have you been hiding something from me over all these years? I know the two of you sometimes move in bohemian circles but I would never have picked you as potential swingers. What am I missing here?"

Harriet stopped speaking and turned and moved over to the stove to attend to the coffee.

Charlotte giggled. It was one of her endearing traits.

"Well, Hetty. There are moments in life when the unthinkable can arrive from out of the blue. All I'm saying is that it is probably good when something like this pops up and gets us thinking about our lives. That's all. End of story. Oh, I should have brought the biscuits I bought yesterday. Macaroons! Delicious!"

Charlotte thought she had made a convincing retraction of any suggestion that she was promoting the idea of participating in some of what the invitation was suggesting. It didn't quite work.

Harriet brought the coffee's over to the bench.

"You know I never like admitting I'm wrong, Lottie. However, now that we are having this conversation, why don't we have some fun and pretend we'd like to get raunchy? What do you think? That would be real secret women's business, wouldn't it?"

Harriet brought out a brown paper bag containing two superb chocolate brownies that she said she'd bought from the patisserie yesterday. She put them on a pretty plate and brought a jug of runny cream from the fridge.

"Hetty! You know I shouldn't eat such things. I so have to watch my weight." Then Charlotte giggled again.

"Not only that. Eating them will definitely make me raunchy."

Harriet almost choked on her first mouthful, laughing loudly.

"Well lets hope they serve these at the party. Or maybe we should take some with us?"

Much laughter followed. Then Charlotte announced that she was feeling hot and once again the two convulsed with laughter. Harriet stared at her gorgeous bespectacled neighbour and allowed herself to imagine Lottie in a different setting; an intimate setting.

"Well darling, I guess there is not a lot you can do about it right now?" Harriet's eyes twinkled, showing slightly more interest in the subject than Charlotte would have thought.

Charlotte moved around the kitchen island bench and slipped an arm around Harriet's waist and looked up at her beautiful friend with her most appealing and seductive smile, and in a timid little voice she announced, "Well in that case, given my susceptibility and the presence of such attractive company, I suppose I would need a tiny grope to settle me down, Hetty."

The silence seemed to go on for ever. Harriet at first looked confused and a blush spread over her face, but then she took on a look that Charlotte had never seen before. She slipped her arm around Charlotte's shoulders and pulled her closer, squeezing her and smiling lovingly down at the irresistible Lottie. Then she reached forward and placed a hand on her neighbour's blouse and whispered; "Will we start with breasts, darling?"

Two naked women lay back on the bed and rested, their eyes closed. Neither wanted to speak first. What they had done together was totally new and both knew it would change their lives for ever.

With her eyes still closed, Harriet reached out and let her hand and fingers caress Charlotte's neck and shoulders.

Charlotte opened her eyes and rolled over and stared at Harriet. Lips joined lips then tongues slipped shyly into mouths and the two woman clasped each other sighing, letting go any tensions they might have felt.

"Are we in love, Lottie?"

"I think so, Hetty. I will want you like this again and again."

"I will want you too, Lottie. I can't remember ever feeling like this. I will want to feel it again."

Charlotte rolled slowly onto Harriet's beautiful body and gyrated on her new love.

"I will always be here for you, my love."

The two bodies convulsed and Harriet called out. "Yes, oh yes!"

It was a fortnight before the big Saturday night party that both the Logans and the Joneses were planning to attend. But before that, the two couples were due for their monthly Friday night dinner at their favourite restaurant, the Cheswick, situated only a short walking distance from their houses.

"I have a plan," Harriet announced.

Lottie and Harriet were having coffee at a cafe in Paddington.

"A plan for what, Hetty?"

"Well Lottie! You remember how we managed to break through with our ideas about swinging?"

"How could I not remember, my love."

"And we know that sharing with others is a positive thing and not a negative thing?

"Well! I think we should try and open up our husbands to these ideas. We don't want them clamping up at the party. We know how men can hang on to fixed beliefs even when there is evidence of a benefit from change.

"I've got a plan that will change them, at least in part."

"And your plan is?"

"You and I are going to swap husbands for a night. We both know that this will lead to change of some sort. Hopefully, when we get to the party, George and Henry will fearlessly embrace the idea of swinging."

Lottie stared at her friend.

"I think you may have forgotten something. You first need to ask me what I think about the idea so that I can choose whether or not to offer my support, perhaps more importantly, my husband."

Harriet sat silently staring at her friend.

"I'm so sorry, darling. That was very bad form on my part. Please accept my sincere apologies."

There was a moment of silence.

"Okay! Apologies accepted. Now what's the plan."

Harriet screamed and grabbed her friend and kissed her.

"That was so bad of me. I should begin again.

"What if we each took home the others husband? It can be discreet as in we need never tell each other what happened, if indeed something did happen.

"The shock of our generosity and openness would be felt by both men. The idea of sharing would be permanently implanted in their brains.

"Now that you and I are lovers, we both want to enjoy greater freedom to express our emotions with others and we need to establish our right to do this earlier rather than later."

The two stared meaningfully at each other.

"So how do we do it, my love. I'm ready."

"Well, the plan is really very simple. We seat the men differently at dinner. George will sit beside you and Henry will be seated beside me.

"When they ask why this is being done, we confess that we are implementing an exercise to better enable a sharing experience in preparation for the party the following fortnight.

"Without much preamble, we tell them that they are being sent home each with a different partner but that they should not be alarmed.

"We will emphasise that there is no pressure for either of them to perform in any way that doesn't take their fancy."

Harriet stopped speaking and smiled at Lottie before going on.

"We will tell them that the woman sitting beside them might freely touch their leg and that in turn, they may touch her leg or legs."

"Then what happens?"

"We then state that at the end of the meal, the two of them should return, not to their own home but to the other mans home. We will leave ahead of them and they should follow twenty minutes or half an hour later. We will be there ready to receive them."

A short silence ensued while Charlotte and Harriet digested what had been said. It all seemed so simple. But it all rested on their husbands agreeing to the plan.

"I must surely have forgotten something, Lottie. It all sounds so simple. Oh yes! We must wear loose skirts or dresses so that if either of them want to become amorous under the table, they don't have to fight their way up a tight skirt."

Charlotte laughed.

"You tend to overthink things Harriet, but in this instance I think its a good thing. We wouldn't want to block a man's efforts, would we, darling. We're offering them something different so they might like our help.

"I remember how I had to go to great lengths to get Henry to touch my bottom. Now he loves it. Oops! Sorry, Hetty. Too much information."

Harriet stared lovingly her Lottie. Then in a little voice she said, "And was it worth it darling?"

Charlotte smiled her special reassuring smile. "It sure was, Hetty."

Harriet smiled, then she came back to the task at hand.

"Now I'm thinking that we should give them more warning. Should we tell them tonight, perhaps?

"Yes! They will need time to think things over. And we should text each other when we've done it so we both know that they know and we are on track."

"Good idea, I'll tell George when we're having a glass of red after dinner. That's the best time to get him. He's more likely to listen then."

"Fine, Hetty! Lets do it. And let's make it fun. We should let our husbands know that sex and love can be separate things, and that with the right outlook on life, everything can be fun for all."

TWO
LOTTIE'S HOLIDAY SECRET

Charlotte and Henry shared a secret. It wasn't that they regretted what happened or about what they did, but talking to others about this particular holiday experience just did not seem appropriate.

Their last caravan journey had led them to Port Douglas, the upmarket coastal resort in northern New South Wales.

They had overlooked the need to book into their usual caravan park. Not only that, they were late getting there after stopping to help another couple with a caravan with a loose wheel problem.

The unusually warm weather ensured that the holiday resort was crowded more than usual and they were turned away from every caravan park.

"Well, darling. I think I'll put on Toby's lucky hat that arrived in the post yesterday. Sure to score a campsite with that on. He said its luck is guaranteed."

Their son, Toby was always sending his mother jokes and things. This time it was a fluffy bunny-rabbit hat.

"This place looks expensive but we'll give it a try." Henry spoke with the air of someone who was about to make a terrible mistake.

"Fingers crossed, darling."

Henry left the car and headed to reception while Charlotte adjusted the ears on her new hat. "Best of luck, sweetheart."

Charlotte watched through the window as the receptionist shook her head, suggesting that they were full and couldn't help. But then she looked out at Charlotte sitting in the car then smiled at Henry and seemed to nod in the affirmative and soon Charlotte watched as Henry proffered his credit card.

"Well, darling! What happened there? It looked from here as though we weren't going to get in."

"Damned if I know. What I do know is that I had to pay for five nights. We have the last available space at the far end of the park. She said that she thought we'd rung and cancelled earlier but I assured her it wasn't us. Anyway! We are joining up with a group called the Bunny Club. They come here twice a year apparently."

Charlotte stared at her husband, speechless.

"What is it darling? Why are you looking at me like that."

Charlotte lifted her hand and pointed a finger at her head.

"Toby was right, darling! My lucky hat! And its a bunny!"

Henry smiled at his beautiful kooky wife. "You'd better keep it on darling. You look gorgeous. You might get especially lucky."

Charlotte slapped his arm. "Promises, promises."

"That reminds me. Lois at the office smiled at me in a funny way and said in almost a whisper that the Port Douglas Swingers would be joining us on Saturday night in the park behind where we are going. I didn't think about it when she mentioned it. Now its got me wondering. What did she mean?"

Henry guided the rig along what seemed like a lonely track between the sandy beach and the tree'd parkland. Suddenly they arrived at a collection of big luxury vans and he quickly discovered Lot 28.

"Wow! So this is where the money hangs out. Bunny Club members obviously enjoy a grand lifestyle. Hope we can fit in, Lottie."

"Whatever it takes, darling! It's such a beautiful spot. I'll do anything to fit in here."

Henry put his hand across and rubbed his wife's knees.

"Even if it means doing whatever it is that Bunny Club members do?"

"Yes, darling. I'll even join the Bunny Club."

They soon had their van positioned and their vehicle parked alongside. The kettle had just boiled when there was a knock on the van wall beside the fly wire door.

Charlotte went to see who it was and discovered an amazing smiling attractive older woman beaming up at her.

"Hello! My name is Caroline. My husband Bertie and I are in that van across from yours. You're the new couple. Glad you made it after all. We heard you'd cancelled.

"I thought I'd just let you know that Fridays is when we have our barbecue and drinks night. Once you've settled in, please come and join us. There will be plenty to eat and drink so unless you want to bring something, feel free to just turn up.

"Oh yes! I nearly forgot. Just wear your nightie or pyjamas. Most of us do. The men usually wear their beach shorts and a t-shirt. The girls love to dress up a little more stylish, if you know what I mean. It makes it more fun for the boys. We love informality."

Charlotte noticed the woman's lipstick and her painted red finger and toe nails and her dyed blond hair. More noticeable though, was her almost see-through robe through which Charlotte viewed a pair of very tiny red bikini-style knickers along with a matching bra.

"Thank you, Caroline. You're very kind. My name is Charlotte - or Lottie - and my husband is Henry. We've had a funny sort of day but plan to take a walk on the beach before bed so maybe we will call in. Hopefully we'll catch up then. Thanks so much for inviting us."

Charlotte moved back into the van and looked at her smiling husband who had been peeping through the side window.

"Wow! Not sure if you've brought the right clothes for this, darling. I might have to represent us on my own. I've got shorts and a t-shirt."

Charlotte feigned to whack him on the shoulder.

"I'm not letting you out of my sight with women like that prowling around. I'm suddenly suspicious of our fellow Bunnies. And what did Lois mean when she said the local Swingers club would be joining the Bunnies tomorrow night? Hmm! Now I think about it, I wonder what Caroline's Bertie is like, just in case Caroline drags you into her luxury van and I'm suddenly all alone."

Henry was busy unlocking the kitchen cupboard safety door catches.

Charlotte watched her husband with interest.

"You sound like you are looking forward to joining the club darling. If they are swingers, then you and I need to agree on what we'll do."

"To swing or not to swing, that is the question. Is it better to suffer alone or with others. Are we true loves happy to be consenting adults and enjoy life's earthly pleasures?"

Charlotte stared hard at Henry, impressed with his soliloquy but also trying to work out which way he was leaning. The nunnery scene of Shakespeare's Hamlet was fine but she hadn't really considered things very seriously up until now. But then she loved him so much that she was sure she would be happy with whatever her husband had in mind.

"I think we'd need to check out the neighbours before we agree to letting things get too warmed up. This could be life changing, darling. You might just find that perfect set of tits I know you've always wanted to get your mouth on."

Henry laughed and slapped his wife's backside.

"Now that's a thought, sweetheart."

"Now I can probably find a little something to slip into which will keep you close to me once the others see what I'm wearing. Why don't you pop out and check the van props before it gets too dark darling, and I'll rummage through my wardrobe."

Henry was still coming to terms with his wife's silk pyjamas and what she wasn't wearing underneath. When he teasingly pulled on the back of her elasticised pants before they left the caravan, he was shocked to see just her superb bare bum.

"Now I know why I have to keep close to you, you sexy little devil."

Charlotte turned on him with her special smile.

"I have a feeling I'll have a lot of competition so I suggest you don't go too far away without my permission. Anything could happen to me."

The loving couple were enjoying their banter and Henry couldn't help himself running his hands over Lottie's silk-covered body as they travelled the few steps to the event.

When Henry and Charlotte appeared from around the corner of Caroline and Bertie's van to join the thirty or more people standing around a gas barbecue, there was a sudden silence before Caroline announced that Lottie and Henry where new Bunnies who had managed to get here after all.

"Henry and Lottie! Welcome! This motley crew meet here for two weeks every year. It is that special time when like-minded folk get away from the humdrum restraints of suburban life."

Voices called out. "Welcome!" and "Nice to meet you both.

"Help yourself to food and drink and just make yourselves at home."

Henry took hold of Lottie's hand and mumbled something to her about the possibility of mistaken identity. Then an amazing looking woman came up to the new arrivals and handed them paper plates.

"You'll find cutlery beside the salads. I'm Lorraine but you don't need to remember names. I'm in the van over there with my mother and sister, Ruth and Greta. We come here every year. Love it! Hope you enjoy yourselves. You're welcome to call over to our van any time if you want to."

Charlotte couldn't help but notice how attentive Lorraine was to Henry and alarm bells rang although she concealed it perfectly from her husband. And there were Lorraine's amazing tits which she thought were most likely false, barely contained inside her two-sizes-too-small racerback tank top. But false or not, it didn't stop Henry ogling them.

As Henry headed for the barbecue, Bertie, Caroline's husband fronted Charlotte holding out two champagne glasses. "You'll need these, I think. Love your outfit! You look gorgeous."

"Thank you," Charlotte mumbled back.

Bertie reached out his hand and caressed her thigh.

"Silk is hard to beat, isn't it? It can take us all to heaven."

Before Charlotte could reply, Caroline replaced Bertie and suddenly the alluring older woman's hand was caressing Charlotte's backside through her silky pyjamas. But the beautiful woman did not stop there. Moments later, Charlotte felt the a hand slide down inside her pants and Caroline lovingly began a gently stroking of a bare buttock. Charlotte was momentarily nonplussed. But then she looked over towards where Henry was loading their plates at the salad bar and was shocked to discover that Lorraine appeared to have her hand firmly placed on her husbands tackle.

Charlotte took a moment to look around and more closely observe what was happening elsewhere and very quickly discovered that all sorts of things were going on.

Charlotte assumed that all of these people had been drinking for a while before she and Henry arrived. Now she could see what was happening and her assumption about alcohol was confirmed.

On the far side of the barbecue a woman was kissing another woman and had a hand firmly placed between the woman's legs. Down past the salad bar, a man was locked in passionate embrace with a woman who he had impaled against a gently rocking caravan wall while behind him, a woman was dragging down his trousers. And when Charlotte's eyes came back to Henry, Lorraine had Charlotte's husband's hand up under her top.

"Do you like me touching your bottom darling? Feel free to touch me anywhere you like, Lottie. I would love it," whispered the attentive Caroline

Suddenly Charlotte was forced to deal with her own situation and now she knew what she wanted most.

"I love what you are doing with your hand Caroline. It feels beautiful. May I kiss you?

The lips of the two women came together and Caroline's hand became rapidly animated between Charlotte's legs, slipping around to her front and fingering her tiny bush.

Charlotte reciprocated, finding her way beneath the woman's robe and into her tiny bikini pants. The two woman gasped and Charlotte found herself experiencing new feelings and beautiful sensations. And then she felt other hands behind her and her pants being drawn down over her bum and lowered to her knees. Bertie's finger was exploring the crack between her buttock cheeks, but then she realised that it wasn't his finger. Bertie let his fat cock rest happily between her buttock cheeks. Charlotte was suddenly on fire.

Charlotte could now focus only on what was happening to her and she judged it all as simply wonderful.

When Henry glanced across at Charlotte, what he saw was sufficient confirmation that his beautiful wife was enjoying herself and most importantly, she appeared to be quite safe. Then he looked into the pleading eyes of Lorraine and smiled.

"Show me your caravan, Lorraine; and I'd love to meet your sister and your mum."

Lorraine joyfully took his hand and led him across to her van and introduced him to her family. They took turns kissing him passionately and surreptitiously clutching his crotch. Then Henry followed three scantily clad ladies up the caravan steps. The view of their almost bare backsides was indeed beautiful.

Henry found himself standing beside a very big bed watching the three hungry women open and then drop his shorts to the ground.

Then Lorraine's mother drew his stiff cock to her mouth and slurped with loud sounds of satisfaction and moments later, she passed him on to the lipsticked lips of her daughters. Then they laid Henry on the bed, removed what clothes they had on, and languidly continued their sucking and sharing in the nude, quietly telling the captured man that he was now their prisoner and that he would never get out alive.

"Lets go to somewhere more private, darling. Hop up into our van. You will find it very comfy."

The soft voice of the beautiful woman fingering her made it easy for Charlotte to willingly do her bidding.

In just moments, Caroline had dragged off both their knickers and straddled her young visitor. Charlotte melted underneath the beautiful humping woman, her hands on Caroline's backside, their pelvic mounds moving in unison and each taking turns to be on top or below the other. And when Charlotte was taking a turn underneath her delightful humping new lady friend she looked up and saw Bertie with his very impressive cock in one hand and what looked like a tube of something in the other.

Seeing a strange cock sent a new thrill down her spine and around her genitals. Charlotte hadn't seen another man's erect private parts in many years. Then she heard Caroline soothing voice.

"Do you do anal darling? That beautiful derriere deserves special attention and my husband craves it, I can see. Can you do him the honour of giving him access? He has lubricant and he'll be very gentle."

Charlotte couldn't answer for a moment. She knew that her rear excited both men and women and the thought of accomodating Bertie there was intriguing. She and Henry had only recently tried doing it. Now she was being given the opportunity to try it with someone else, someone experienced.

"Yes I have tried it, and yes I would like Bertie to have his way with it. Just so long as you stay with me, Caroline.

Caroline looked up at Bertie and smiled.

"The darling girl is offering you access, Bertie. She is not very experienced. She's not quite an anal virgin but please be gentlemanly about it. This is not one of your skinny anal harlots Esme and her sister Candice, back home, waiting for you to walk through the door and ravish their arses. I'll be watching."

Charlotte had listened carefully to her lady lover's conversation and she immediately felt safe and excited. She also took note of what was said about anal harlots and for some reason she found the idea exciting.

"Role over on your tummy, Lottie, and lift yourself up onto your knees. I think Bertie should give your pussy a little shag before he goes near your other place. It will get your juices properly running."

Charlotte was already excited and even more so listening to her older lady-love. She rolled over and lifted herself up and it was only moments later that the first cock since she married Henry, twenty four years ago, was lovingly exploring her very wet cunt.

"That looks so good, Bertie. I'll fondle your testicles as a reward.

"And Lottie, I do hope you are enjoying being a member of the Bunny

Club. I hope you like my husbands cock. I love sucking and playing with cocks and Bertie has lots of friends here with lovely cocks so if you ever want more of them, just say.

"Bertie sometimes organises a mini gang bang for me when he thinks I need a bit of a lift. I find four is a good number."

Charlotte felt Caroline putting the squeegee against her anus. Then she felt the cool liquid and her lovers finger gently probing the freshly lubricated little orifice.

"I think she's ready, Bertie. Give me your cock."

Charlotte felt Bertie exiting, then she felt his knob being rubbed against her butt hole. Then Caroline eased her husbands stiff member into Charlotte's bottom where it rested, giving Charlotte time to adjust. Then Caroline took Bertie out while she added more lubricant. She returned him to Charlotte's butt hole and told Bertie to "give it to her slowly, darling" and Bertie did.

Charlotte had so often wondered what it would be like to have her arse fucked before she and Henry had discovered it. Now she was finding out what a different cock was like, discovering that she adored it. To have a big beautiful object sliding right in and then backing out of her slippery bum hole was beautiful beyond her wildest imagination.

In those first few moments with Bertie and his wife serving her, Charlotte knew that she would want this sort of thing regularly in her life. And she also realised something else. She would be a swinger, maybe even an anal harlot, and watching her husband go off with Lorraine she knew her darling Henry would swing with her.

When Charlotte awoke mid morning, Henry was curled up asleep beside her.

She first thought she should get up and open the curtains but then she changed her mind.

Instead she pushed back the quilt and took her husbands cock in her hand. It was shrivelled and felt very soft and when she put her face down to touch it with her tongue, she inhaled the strong odour of other women and this excited her and she wished they were there in the bed so that she could touch them.

As she gently kissed and sucked Henry and palmed her pussy, her mind wandered to all that had happened the evening before and she suddenly trembled with excitement as those actions, images and sensations were revisited.

Then she thought about Henry and wondered if he had enjoyed swinging as much as she had.

Charlotte pondered their immediate situation along with their future together. She loved her husband dearly, so how does one reconcile that love and her desire to enjoy other lovers?

Henry's cock twitched in Charlotte's mouth. Then she felt her husbands hand on her back and he lovingly caressed her.

"I love you, Lottie."

"I love you, Henry. Are we now happy swingers, sweetheart?"

"I believe we are, darling. We are a very lucky couple."

"I think I'd like to swing again, Henry."

"Tonight sounds like it could be good for that, Charlotte."

"Yes my love. And Henry?"

"Yes, darling?"

"I do love the smell and taste of last nights ladies on your cock."

Her loving attention to Henry's cock had brought him to the ready and Charlotte thought she would try something.

"Darling! I know you are probably very tired but if you lay back and I climb up and lower my bottom onto you, will you let me give you a loving anal fuck?"

"I would love that, Lottie my love, and if you don't mind, I might come in your beautiful bum? Let's do it."

THREE

TIME TO CHANGE

"We should let our husbands know that sex and love can be separate things, and that with the right outlook on life, everything can be enjoyed by all."

That message echoed in Harriet's brain as she attempted to find the words with which she would tell George about their plan. He was already home and in the shower and she knew that crunch time was looming.

The doorbell sounded and George collected the Thai takeaway.

George came from the kitchen carrying a tray with the food. Mini spring rolls, yellow curry with tofu and a large bowl of coconut rice.

"Have you had a good day, George? Mine was good. Sold two complete full-width floor to ceiling window sets, plus we had an inquiry about curtains and blinds for four new appartments."

George nodded."Very good. Ours was pretty standard. Nothing big. Just a couple of sails and a jib resulting from last months heavy weather."

Harriet felt weak in the stomach. Why had she thought that this was a good idea. Ursula's bloody party wasn't that important. But then she remembered cuddling up to Lottie and wondered what proper full swinging freedom might be like.

"George?"

"Yes, darling."

"I've got something to tell you. I've been talking to Lottie about the party that we are attending in a couple of weeks."

George sipped his drink then looked at his wife.

"And?"

"Well as you know, it is an adult party which means that people can chat-up other people if they feel so inclined. Well, Lottie and I have agreed that we should open up a little, not necessarily to run amuck on party night, but just to be less inhibited by what other people might do."

George stared at his wife with a bemused look on his face.

"And?"

"Well. Lottie came up with the idea that we should swap partners for the night after our monthly dinner at the Cheswick on Friday. Nothing in particular needs to happen, darling. We just think it would make us more aware of how some of the other party guests might think and feel."

George was transfixed.

"And?"

Harriet was reminded how her husband was a man of few words, especially when he was involved in a business deal or a situation where he would need to take the lead in decision making.

"Well, darling. We figured that on Friday night we would simply change our seating arrangement so that you sat beside Charlotte and I sat beside Henry. Then when we'd eaten, she and I would bid you farewell and head home. You two would enjoy your drinks and follow us home half-an-hour later.

"And?"

"You would go across the road to the Logan's house and Henry would come here to our house."

"And?"

Harriet knew that having come this far, there was no going back.

"Well, darling. What we all do is probably going to be very little. Both residences have spare rooms and beds. Once you have arrived at your destination, you and Lottie work out the rest of the evening and myself and Henry will do the same, here."

Harriet was feeling decidedly uncomfortable, even a little sick in the stomach. What had she done? What would George say or do? And why was he staring at her like that?

"Okay! What time do we come back home?"

Harriet was dismayed though she was just able to hide her surprise. She and Lottie hadn't discussed this. It didn't seem relevant.

"Er, well, um I guess we should discuss that right now. When would you think you would want to come back, darling?"

"Well I usually like to sleep-in on Saturdays, as you know. How about 10am."

Again Harriet was dismayed. George was treating the whole affair so casually that it seemed like he was simply going away for a golfing weekend with his mates.

"Okay, darling. I'll mention that to Lottie so that she doesn't blast you out of bed with loud music when she rises at six to do the washing."

Harriets attempt at irony worked and her husband burst into laughter.

"I'm enjoying my night away already, sweetheart, and I haven't even left the house. I take it that you two will have swapped Henry and my pyjamas and dressing gown during the day so neither of us will need to worry about that."

Harriet was emotionally rung out but the more George laughed about it the more relaxed she became.

"Well, I think you've taken this plan to heart, darling and I'm very thankful. I'll clear these dishes then I'll text Lottie and tell her you've agreed.

"Oh yes, there is one other thing that I forgot to mention. At dinner, us girls will have the right to touch the men on the leg, a simple reminder of our goodwill. Thank you, darling."

As Harriet was leaving with the dishes, George called out.

"Can the blokes touch the girls legs?"

Harriet stopped at the doorway and called back.

"Of course, darling. Isn't that what girls legs are for?"

Over the road at the Logan house, Henry had brought home a roast chicken and Lottie had steamed some vegetables. She had also made her wonderful bread and butter pudding which she knew her husband loved, and as he started on a second helping, Lottie sprung the house swap message on him.

"Sweetheart, I need to tell you about something Hetty and I have cooked up to loosen George up before the swinger party."

Charlotte went on to tell Henry about the plan to send he and George home to their neighbours houses after their Friday night monthly dinner to try to get George loosened up before Ursula's swinger party.

"Hetty doesn't know anything about what we've been doing on our caravan adventures, Henry and it would be best if we never mentioned it. However, my dearest love, I will tell you that she and I have this past week made a breakthrough in the feely-touchy area, but again, please don't say a word. She wants to swing, I'm certain of it, but she's very wary and self-conscious about it."

Charlotte lead her husband into the lounge room and Henry took is true love by the hand and kissed it.

"You forever surprise me, my love. You know I'll be fine with it and unless she wants me to do something, I'm quite happy to snuggle up in the spare bedroom."

Charlotte smiled lovingly at him.

"Well, I've told you how the girls might put their hands on the blokes legs and it's okay for the blokes to respond if they want to.

"Now I could say more, or perhaps I should stop there. But if a little bird whispered that another little bird was interested in some naughty person taking an interest in her rear-end, then that might be useful information for some person stuck in a house across the road and far from home."

Henry roared laughing and grabbed his wife and pulled her across his knee and lifted her skirt. Charlotte wriggled her bum provocatively.

"One little bird at a time, me thinks, starting with this one."

As her husband attempted to draw down her draws, Lottie squirmed and protested but just a little too much.

And after the two eventually exhausted themselves on the sofa and the carpet, Henry asked if he would need to pack a little bag for his trip across the road.

"I will look after everything my love. Even your pyjama's will be waiting for you. I'll even send you off with a small tube of lube."

Henry looked lovingly at his wife. Then he put his hand between her legs and rubbed her gently. Then, in a quiet voice he mentioned the house swap plan.

"Make sure you keep some lube on hand, my love. You will probably need it. This little bird knows that another little bird has admired your rear-end. Need I say more?"

Lottie swung herself on to her man.

"Oh dear. My poor derriere just attracts attention wherever it goes. I just don't know what to do."

The loving couple hugged and squeezed each other.

"Is there any more bread and butter pudding, darling?"

FOUR

HAPPY BIRTHDAY BERTIE

It was a warm balmy spring day as Charlotte met up with Caroline at the caravan park kiosk. The two smiled warmly, both genuinely pleased to see each other. Their interactions had been memorable and each carried a desire to explore each other further.

"Lets have a coffee out under the trees, shall we?"

Over short blacks and a shared brownie the two chatted about the weather and how they were enjoying the deep sleep they were experiencing on their beach holiday. Then Caroline put a question to Lottie.

"Lottie? I'm giving Bertie his birthday present at around four-o'clock and I'd love it if you could be there. You might even like to help me with his gift."

Charlotte smiled at the sexy older woman. Even in her plain clothes, Jeans and a check shirt, Caroline exuded an allure that was simply too hard to ignore.

"Love to, Caroline. Is it something you know he likes, or will it be a complete surprise."

Caroline offered a smile as though she were about to reveal a secret.

"Well, he's been getting it every year for a long time and he never tires of it. I only give it to him on his birthday or occasionally when I think he deserves something special. Mind you, I secretly enjoy it as much as he does."

Something about what the woman had said intrigued Charlotte and she wanted to know more.

"Yes, Caroline. I'd love to come to his birthday. Can I ask what it is you will be giving him? I sense its a tiny bit risqué"

Caroline laughed loudly.

"I wouldn't invite you if it wasn't, Charlotte. You will be one of the candles on his cake, so to speak. You, and probably a couple of older women from the Boner Bitches club should keep him going for quite a while.

"I'm giving him his favourite, a good hard pegging. The other women there will be enjoying the performance. They will want to enjoy him too. They do love it that he gets such a big erection when he's pegged."

Charlotte was confused.

"I don't know what pegging is, Caroline. Sounds exciting. Please enlighten me."

"Oh you are so sweet, darling. Pegging is when a woman puts her strap-on dildo up a man's arse and shags him. Actually, it doesn't have to be a man. Us girls do it to each other, too.

"Amazingly, most men either don't know about it or don't want to know. They are the ones who have yet to discover the wonderful feelings that are derived from their prostate gland and available to them via their anus.

"A bonus for the ladies is that a man gets a very substantial erection from a good pegging which we can use to our advantage. Win-win all round, don't you think?"

Charlotte couldn't believe what she was hearing. How was it that she had never heard of it given that the idea was so exciting? Then she realised Caroline was talking again and quickly tuned in.

"I usually dress up for him. Garter belt, stockings and heels. The Boner Bitches usually do, too. We all love being his fantasy women.

"I've plenty of dress up lingerie stuff if you want to look through it. You don't have to though. Just come as you like. You might not keep much on for long anyway. I also have a large collection of strap-ons you can choose from, too. You will love it, I'm sure.

"You will be the youngest. The other ladies will try to take advantage of you, I'm sure but just say 'no thank you' if anyone tries something you're not comfortable with. They won't be offended.

"Please come, Charlotte. I was quite envious of my husband when you let him in the other day. Come and let me introduce you to pegging. You'll love it, darling."

Charlotte was thinking fast but it didn't take long for her to confirm her acceptance of the invitation.

"I'll definitely be there, Caroline."

"Bertie has gone fishing with his mates this morning so he'll be getting his present around 4pm, after he's showered and prepared himself.

"If you would like to come over around 3pm, you could meet the ladies and try on stuff if you wish. I can also show you a range of dildo's. I would recommend a small one to start with. Once you get the hang of it you can try something bigger."

Charlotte said she'd be there at three o'clock.

"Tell me more about the Boner Bitches, Caroline. Who are they and why are they called that?"

"Oh yes. I'm a member. It's sub-branch of the East Sydney Swingers Club. It's mostly middle aged and older women who either have husbands who like it or need it to get an erection. Or they are may have lost a partner so enjoy inviting others over for scones and tea and bending each other over the arm of the settee to get their parts thoroughly reamed. They find they are in high demand with widowers and widows alike.

"It's not that she isn't powerful without a dildo but it's different, and the feeling she gets shagging a man or a woman's backside is just wonderful. I hope you will find it so, darling. So maybe, like me, they just love the feeling a woman experiences when she gets herself a cock."

Charlotte arrived at her new friends huge caravan at three as arranged. Caroline welcomed her and invited her into the lounge.

"Come and meet some old friends, darling."

Charlotte smiled happily as she was introduced first to Janice, the tallest longest legged and thinest woman Charlotte had ever met, and Mary, a woman with a voluptuous figure best described as rubenesque.

Their faces were carefully made up to look overly sluttish and both wore stockings and high heels and their skirts were short allowing Charlotte to view their stocking tops and suspender clips.

"Now, my favourite whores! This is Lottie who I've told you about. And yes, she is gorgeous as you can see but please don't rush the girl. There will be plenty of time to get to know each other later. Right now she will be checking out my dress-up draws and looking at my range of toys."

Caroline ushered Charlotte into the bedroom and opened the doors of a large walk-in wardrobe. She pulled open a draw full of underwear then asked Charlotte if it would be easier if she picked out things she thought would look good and pass them to her. Charlotte agreed.

"I don't think I will be able to look as sexy as you lot so perhaps I should go for something more conservative, Caroline. Oh yes, those tiny knickers do look good don't they? And yes, maybe a garter belt with jiggly bits hanging down, just for decoration. And yes! Coffee-coloured hold-ups would look good with those medium heeled bone sandals."

Moments later, Caroline opened her sex-toy draw and Charlotte faced a whole knew world of adult playthings.

"Now keeping things simple would be the way to go."

Caroline picked up a pink rubber cock and handed it to Charlotte. "Thats a standard old-style six-and-a-half inch dick, darling. It's good for everything but most of us have moved on to newer less male-centric models. Caroline held up a long thin blue cylindrical object. We could give you this thinner one designed specifically for gentler anal penetration. A woman still gets a buzz from using it exactly as she would with a bigger one. Please yourself, Lottie."

Charlotte deliberated for a moment, then made her decision.

"I think I'll take my chances with a bigger one, Caroline. I always feel that there are times in life when you should just jump into the deep end. I'm thinking this is one of them."

They looked through the many shapes and colours together and Caroline selected a clear perspex model with multi-coloured glitter.

"Gosh, Caroline. Do you get these out for table decorations at Christmas?"

They laughed and Caroline hugged her young protege.

"You are going to be a very busy little lady today, I can see that."

When the two returned to the lounge, a new person had arrived.

"Tanya! This is Charlotte but you can call her Lottie. She is one of the resident campers here. It's her first time at the swingers site so be gently with her. Lottie? This creature who can offer more than enough to everybody is Tanya."

Charlotte wanted to stare at the new arrival but managed not to. Tanya was what anyone being a little unkind would call a fatty. And her outfit exaggerated every aspect of her body. She wore a loose robe over her delectable's but then in a fit of giggles, she opened the robe and called everyone's attention to her new bra.

"Just arrived. In my size at last! Hope you like it?"

Tanya's bra was big black and beautiful. But the attention grabbing feature were the large holes for the nipples and their immediate surrounds. Both nipples stood out, screaming for a mouth or fingers. The women staring at her were quick to respond.

Mary, who Charlotte thought was a little on the heavy side too, got to Tanya first, pushing her against the wall and fastening her teeth to the left nipple. Janice was only seconds behind and claimed mouthing rights to the right breast.

Not to be left out, Caroline took Charlotte by the hand, leading her down onto the floor where Charlotte watched as Caroline embraced one of Tanya's stocky stockinged legs and groped her way up until she reached the woman's crotch. Then Caroline turned and gestured to Charlotte to take the other leg.

As Charlotte reached out and began to hug the woman's huge warm soft thigh and rub her fingers all over it, she saw Tanya's hands reach down and push down her knickers to make herself more easily available to whoever wanted more of her down below.

Charlotte heeded the invitation and suddenly, she and Caroline were taking turns burying their fingers inside Tanya's huge wet vulva, kissing and tonguing each other as they did so.

Up higher, the two Boner Bitches, Janice and Mary, were about to lead the excited gasping giggling wobbling Tanya to the bedroom, telling her in low voices that every part of her was going to go to heaven.

But suddenly a man's voice interrupted everyone.

"Have I got the wrong day? Don't let me stop you ladies, I'm really enjoying watching you. Maybe this is part of my present?"

"Bertie! Oh darling, I'm so sorry. Things sort of got out of hand. Come down here darling and hold this while I prepare your birthday surprise. Come along girls, get yourselves ready."

Suddenly, Charlotte was kneeling opposite the birthday boy and their hands were sharing a very wet hairy pussy.

"Hello Lottie. So good to see you here. Glad you could join us for my birthday. I know you will make it even more exciting for me."

Then he reached a spare hand across and groped her breasts.

Under less extraordinary circumstances, Charlotte would have made Bertie desist. But with her body already wracked with excitement, the birthday boy's busy fingers nipping her nipples just added to the sexual tension that she was feeling and she found herself thinking about men's cocks alongside all the other stuff that was fighting for her attention.

Amid the confusion, and on a sudden whim, Charlotte pushed her hand up behind her gasping giggling new friend and found Tanya's bottom crack which separated Tanya's buttocks and in a flash, she had two fingers anally anchored.

Tanya gave a huge shudder and smiled lovingly down at the crouching provider of such a loving feeling.

"Don't forget me darling. Give it to me later, sweetheart."

A voice from the bedroom called out to Bertie.

"Bertie, darling, it's birthday time. Come in here and bring those horny sluts with you. Don't keep us waiting darling."

The three emerged from the lounge to a bedroom setting promising an opportunity to follow a truly lustful path. Two double beds crammed in together, were clearly there for fun and games.

"Now first, Bertie, I want you to take off all your clothes and sit here on this upright chair.

"When you're done, each of our guests want to take turns and come and sit on your knee and kiss you and fondle your boy thingy and let you fondle and caress them in any way you want.

"There's no rush darling. The ladies each have five minutes to play with you. We are all here to make sure you enjoy yourself and the ladies agree that there are no limits to what you can ask for.

"When that is all done, I want you to come and kneel on the bed in readiness for your present."

Charlotte looked at a vision splendid. Four delicious fantasy ladies sitting on the edge of the bed in a line - five ladies including herself - all in a state of undress and oozing sexuality. She just wished she was Bertie and have the women sit on her lap.

"Now girls! Bertie is already in the buff and dare I say, from what I can see from here, he's starting to look pretty positive about things. At least a part of him is. So get to it, girls. And you have just five minutes with him. A bell will ring."

Janice was the first to join Bertie. He welcomed the long-legged well-wisher with a hug, and while she wished him a happy birthday and kissed him lovingly, Bertie's hands were immediately on her long silk stockinged legs and her thighs. She willingly responded by opening her legs and his hand travelled up to her pussy, fondling it gently.

Janice wasted no time in grasping Bertie's already rigid cock, moving her hand lovingly up and down.

Then the bell rang and Mary replaced Janice on Bertie's lap.

Again the hugging and kissing and then while Mary clutched Bertie's rigid member and reached under his testicles looking for his anus, Bertie bared her breasts and sucked on a nipple.

Then the bell rang and Tanya replaced Mary on Bertie's lap.

Tanya giggled and waddled over. But instead of sitting on Bertie's lap, she lifted him and sat down on the chair and pulled him down onto her huge lap and hugged and kissed him. Her colourful cock pushed up between Bertie's legs and he took hold of it and waved it around, joyfully calling out, "hopefully, I'll see you later."

Then the bell rang and Charlotte replaced Tanya on Bertie's lap.

They hugged and kissed and Bertie fondled Lottie's thighs and tugged at the flapping elastic suspenders. Then while Lottie closed her eyes and held onto his pleasure wand, Bertie managed to get the end of a finger into her tight little anus.

Then the bell rang and Bertie's wife replaced Charlotte on Bertie's lap, taking hold of his twitching member.

"Now darling. Enough philandering with these whores. Your darling wife wants you on your knees on the bed, please. It's time for your present."

"So lets pop on our pleasure sticks. Once you are strapped up, we'll be ready to play.

Charlotte joined the ladies as each reached behind to where they had hidden their strap-ons, and in a very short time, five colourful cocks in various shapes bobbed up and down and swung from side to side.

All eyes were on Caroline's black multi-bubbled dildo and Bertie's rear end. And when Caroline pushed into her kneeling husbands well lubricated bottom hole and he gasped, they all let out a cheer and yelled, "Happy birthday, Bertie."

Everyone watched the birthday couple for a few minutes. Most reached a hand forward and stroked Caroline's beautiful naked rear end. But then they all looked at each other, thinking about what they were now free to do. All would soon be happy doing loving things with any one of the others, but there was no doubt that Charlotte was in everyones thoughts

Charlotte was suddenly surrounded by waving cocks and she immediately decided to go with the flow, reaching out and squeezing and tugging the ladies lollipop-like 'boners'. They responded with enthusiastic and excited groping and kissing, both of her and each other.

As she grasped Janice's boner and leant forward to kiss her enticing mouth, the woman whispered to her.

"Our van is parked on lot 17, Lottie. Call by tomorrow at around three. Mary and I would love that. Oh, and Lottie. Feel free to bring that hunk of a husband with you. My friend Ruth said she and her daughters could have played with him forever."

Charlotte heart beat faster. Janice was the woman she was most attracted to and whose body she most wanted to explore and she quickly whispered back.

"I'll be there, Janice, and I should be able to entice Henry along."

Caroline looked up at the bevy of beauties.

"Don't get too carried away over there. And don't forget who's birthday it is, girls. Bertie will want his cock checked regularly, and you know he's able to mount anyone who would like to fuck him, back or front.

"You will have to take turns. I can turn him over for hand and mouth jobs or you can duck underneath and get his full attention on your rear end. Who's first?"

Mary scrambled across and lay on her belly beneath Bertie. Then she pushed herself upward and reached back and guided Bertie's huge cock into her pussy, while the others all clapped and called out "bravo, Mary. Go gal."

Everyone watched excitedly as Mary gasped and grunted, moving her significant backside up and down to match Bertie's movements, and it wasn't long before she cried out and collapsed onto her belly.

Caroline paused but then continued her pegging.

"Whose next? Three or four minute's each, to start with."

Charlotte moved forward and quickly repeated what she'd seen Mary do, except she guided Bertie's cock to her bum, not her pussy.

Charlotte was still remembering Bertie's first visit between her buttocks and she desperately wanted to recapture that exquisite feeling. And she wasn't disappointed. But then Caroline called "times up" Lottie, and Charlotte removed herself. She thought how she was going to have to find a way to make this anal thing a part of her regular routine. She wasn't going to want to live without it.

Mary and Janice helped Charlotte back onto the nearby bed, and Mary went behind her and felt around and spread her buttocks. Then she gently inserted the end of her strap-on into Charlotte who pushed back vigorously, leaning over to Janice, to join her mouth to hers. Charlotte's bum's first time with a "boner" lady was like discovering a magic wand and she wanted to cry.

Charlotte and the others watched as Tanya took Bertie's tool in her pussy. Then she screamed and came, shaking her rolls of fat like a dog just leaving the water. Everyone cheered.

Janice chose a different position. She enjoyed seeing and showing off her long legs. She laid on her back and pushed up her abdomen so that Bertie could find her bum while her legs stood high up on either side of the thrusting birthday boy for all to admire.

Caroline let go of Bertie's hips to hold Janice's beautiful ankles and feet high in the air. Then she smothered Janice's stockinged legs with kisses and fingered her ankle straps, pounding Bertie even harder as she did so.

"Give it to her, Bertie. Show the leggy bitch how much you love her birthday present."

All present had enjoyed Bertie from below. Now Caroline removed her dildo and turned Bertie over and reinserted it and continued her gentle thrusting. All present took turns fondling and sucking him. Eventually, the time came to end the birthday celebrations.

"Just one last thing, Bertie my love."

Caroline withdrew from Bertie and removed her strap-on. Then she slid beneath him.

"Time to give your darling wife her present, you beautiful stud. When you are ready of course."

Caroline rolled onto the bed and Bertie dutifully mounted her

Everyone cheered and clapped and suddenly Bertie yelled and his wife threw herself upwards and yelled and the audience clapped. Then turned to each other, and smiled, ready to share more loving fun.

FIVE

AT LAST!

The Logan's and the Jones's sat down in their favourite horseshoe alcove table at their favourite restaurant. But tonight things were a little different.

Charlotte and Harriet sat together in the middle whilst Harriet's husband, George sat next to Charlotte. Henry took the seat beside Harriet. Nothing was said about the new seating arrangement other than Charlotte exclaiming, "Well this is cosy."

Reading the menu took very little time and all had soon ordered starters along with instructions for their main courses. Then Henry led the conversation.

"Well, I'm quite looking forward to Ursula's party. I'm sure there will be people who we know but who we rarely see. And it will be fun seeing who is attracted to who."

Him speaking eased the slight tension among them, moving the focus away from their new seating arrangement.

"Yes, it could be quite funny but then there might be a few shocks. Who knows? I might get off with a tattooed ladyboy from Bondi. This is all about us expanding our horizons, isn't it?"

There was general laughter. But then Harriet put her bit in.

"Well if you do, darling, and you start bringing him – I mean her – home, don't expect me to do her washing."

Again, everyone laughed.

The two women were now finding it a little hard to relax and given that they had planned to make the evening fun and sexy, neither knew what to do next.

Any hand moves under the table seemed too obvious and stilted. At the last minute, the two had gone to the bathroom and removed their knickers, popping them into their handbags. Now, sitting there with bare fanny's, they felt more juvenile than seductive. Charlotte attempted to save the day.

"I think I'd be looking for a very bald man so that I could check those stories about bald men being super-virile."

There was silence, then Harriet came up with a comment.

"One of the ladies who works for George says her very bald husband is extremely satisfying."

George looked across at his wife.

"Who on earth is that, Hetty? I'll call her into the office and ask her for more details."

"No way, darling. I'll never tell you. The poor thing would be mortified."

The waiter arrived with plates of hors d'oevres and everyone began to nibble and sip their glasses of wine.

By the time the diners had started their main courses, enough wine had been consumed to in part, deaden the inhibitions of the party members. Both women had bravely managed to place a hand on the thigh of the man next to them and, encouragingly, both had felt fingers exploring their thighs.

By the time the main course was cleared away and the diners were waiting for deserts, both women were receiving the attention they had hoped for. And they also found themselves giving more attention to their male companions.

When Charlotte had ventured to put her hand on George's crotch, he responded very quickly, pushing his hand to the top of her leg, discovering to his shock and delight, her fluffy pussy, already wet and welcoming.

Harriet's pussy came under a delightful campaign of gentle rubbing when Henry, too, discovered her knicker-less offering. And in her excitement, Harriet fumbled at Henry's zip and with a little help from him, managed to make available to her exited finger tips, only the shiny engorged head of his cock.

The four were fully aware of the situation and the excitement and when they collected themselves in preparation for a quick coffee followed by their departure for boudoir antics at home, each smiled lovingly at each other and agreed that life was good.

"Now, dearest loves, Charlotte and I will leave you shortly. Give us time to get ourselves home and settled, maybe a half or three quarters of an hour. We will expect you any time after that. And please remember where you are supposed to be going."

The two men laughed, knowing that Harriet was referring to them having drunk more than they intended and the possibility they might forget the arrangement.

As the super-attractive and somewhat excited Charlotte and Harriet put on their jackets and said their farewells, two sets of eyes from a table on the far side of the room were watching them. There was nothing in our heroin's plans that would have foretold the dangers of leaving their slightly inebriated partners unattended.

Henry and George were collecting themselves together, stepping back from their excited activities of the past hour or two and trying to focus on the next stage of things. Both were a little the worse for wear.

"George, my old friend? If you are in anyway unhappy with our wives plan, say so, mate. I'm more than happy to back off. I don't want to do anything that would damage our friendship."

There was a sort of muffled silence as George attempted to focus.

"Henry. You are very dear to me and for that reason I'm most happy for you to go and poke my wife. I hope in return, you're granting me a chance to do the same with your missus, our friendship will become a bond for life. Hic!"

It was at that point, in the midst of male bonding and expressions of love and endearment that a gentle voice in front of their table spoke.

"Gentleman. May we join you?"

George and Henry looked up and tried to focus. In front of them stood two very well dressed older, and extremely thin women with angelic smiles.

Please! Be our guests.

The two thin ladies in floral dresses and heeled sandals, sat themselves one either side of the two men, where Charlotte and Harriet had sat.

"I'm Esme and this is my sister Candice. We live nearby. We've noticed that you come here on the last Friday of the month with your wives. Your ladies seem to have left you alone this evening? That is dangerous indeed for two fine looking men like you."

Both men felt a hand on the top of their legs. Then hands lifted each man's hand and dragged it on to a woman's leg. The two surrendered to the womens advances.

When first George and then Henry felt fingers exploring their zippers, they both, without a second thought moved their hands on the ladies boney knees. They slid them up under their dresses and lovingly caressed their skinny but warm shapely thighs. And only moments later both men felt a hand helping to move their fingers up to the woman's knickers and to be pressed against silky warm wet patches.

Two lipsticked doe-eyed sex hungry older woman stared at the men, their smiling open mouths defying them to back away.

"Why don't we go for a walk in the gardens, boys, Candice whispered."

"Or our apartment is just across the street if you would like a nightcap?" echoed the soft voice of her sister.

Getting from the restaurant to Esme and Candice's apartment seemed to take forever but it was really only a few minutes. Once outside, the two women giggled and wanted to play. They took the men by the hand and pulled them away from the bright fairy lights suspended in the trees, leading them behind the large rhododendron bushes and flinging their arms around them and kissing mouth to mouth most energetically. But when George or Henry tried to grope or touch them or put their hands inside their clothes, the women laughed and called out, "Not yet, naughty boys."

But then the ladies slowed and took George and Henry's hands and led them across the road to their ground floor home and within moments, they had removed the mens clothes, lifted their cotton dresses up over their heads and were kneeling on the sofa side by side calling to the men to come and touch them.

George and Henry were still a little groggy and desperately tried to focus but the ladies were so quick, and the affect of the alcohol was slow to dissipate.

The view of Esme and Candice was extraordinary. They both were tanned all over and though they were very skinny, their bodies were as alluring as their smiles.

They turned to the confused men and handled them and gobbled excitedly on their cocks. Then they giggled and looked up at the men's faces.

"We share everything so please enjoy both of us. And we should mention that we love getting it in the back door, so to speak. There is plenty of lube in the basket on the little table.

"Take your time. We can enjoy ourselves while you work out what you want. Oh yes! And we like to be bitten on our tiny tits, too. Anything you want, really. You are with a couple of horny mega hungry bitches. Take advantage. You might never get it this good again."

George and Henry rallied and took hold of a set of hips each. Then they plowed the ladies delicious pussies. Then they put lube on their bums and plowed the ladies tight tiny backsides. Then they swapped ladies and repeated what they had just done.

Esme and Candice screamed and groaned and wriggled and laughed and pushed and occasionally they would have an orgasm, but it did not slow them down.

Then they made the two men kneel on the sofa and produced and attached two dildos. Henry agreed to be pegged by Esme and George watched fascinated, all the while stroking the cock worn by the gasping sighing Candice with one hand while gently stroking her pussy with the other.

When the time came to say goodbye, and they were at the door, the sisters hugged the two men and rubbed themselves against them and invited them to stay longer. Esme handed George a business card with their contact details.

"We've enjoyed ourselves very much, gentlemen. Thank you. Call us or text if you want more loving from the insatiable sisters.

"We're really very loving and will happily take you in hand again."

Two tired men sauntered down the road in silence, each trying to sort out their thoughts.

"What will we do, Henry? I'm totally confused."

There was silence as the two drew close to their houses.

"I know what you mean, George."

After a few minutes, Henry laughed.

"Its been a good night for us, George. Lets not loose momentum. The girls got us started on this journey, wanting us to develope other ways of looking at life. And I think you would agree with me that they've succeded. They didnt allow that we might discover some things on our own.

"I'm thinking that even though it's very late, we just do what they asked and turn up, and hopefully they will be asleep and we just hop into a spare bed and get some sleep.

"In the morning, they might be so pleased to see us home and safe, they won't give us a hard time."

George agreed.

"You are right, Henry. Fuck it! I'm really tired, so lets get some sleep. We'll worry about the girls tomorrow."

Henry stopped walking and George stopped too.

"What is it Henry?"

"I just thought of something, George. We could always say that we thought they arranged to send Esme and Candice to us. That we thought it was just part of their plan. I mean, we can claim that we thought that them leaving early without us was a ruse to leave us with the other women."

George stared at Henry.

"Brilliant, Henry! Let them explain their way out of that. Wow! I feel almost ready to go back for more of those skinny chicks."

Henry laughed.

"Steady, George. You might need to save your energy for my wife. And yours could be out to get answers. Lets tread warily. And George?"

"Yes, Henry?"

"Whatever happens, don't loose that card."

Two women in two houses woke up to the sun streaming through the windows.

In each house, a beautiful scantily clad lady tip-toed into the adjoining bedroom and stared at a man sleeping peacefully. Then they wandered to the kitchen and made coffee and texted each other.

"Hi! Are you okay? George is fast asleep in the spare room. Call whenever you like."

Moments later a return text arrived. "Your husband is asleep in the spare room. I'll call now."

Harriet called Charlotte. "I wonder what happened, Lottie? He seems totally out of it like he had a heavy night. I guess I should just leave him be."

"My thoughts too, darling. I can only think that they got drunk somewhere. My other thought is one that we didn't reckon on. Suppose they got picked up by some other women?"

Harriet laughed.

"Well, it might serve us right if they did. Even I can't think of every possibility."

The two laughed which helped to offset their tension.

"Well, darling, I have a suggestion."

"What is that, Hetty?"

"The sniff test! Every woman leaves an aroma. And darling, if the sniff test comes up positive, we must be ready to fuck the blokes silly so they know where they are really better off."

"Love it, Hetty. We can punish them later if we feel we need to."

· · ·

Harriet waited until after mid morning before she went to check on Henry. He had rolled over but was still asleep. She went and gently pulled back the bed clothes. Henry had removed his trousers and under pants and he lay there with a large but flaccid cock.

Harriet lifted it and put her face down and sniffed it. Yes, indeed, there was a strong smell of a woman and sex.

Harriet put the bed clothes back and went and fetched a bath towel and laid it on the bed. Then she left and returned to the kitchen.

As she entered, a text arrived.

"A very interesting aroma on his cock. How about you?"

Harriet texted back.

"Same story here. I've left a bath towel on the bed for him to find when he wakes up. We might have company for longer than we expected."

Over at Charlotte's house, George was totally naked in the spare bed. After she had read the latest text from across the road, she did the same and fetched a bath towel and laid it on the bed. Then she too, returned to the kitchen.

Both women had time to think about things, and unbeknown to each other, they came to the same decision.

When a scrubbed-up Henry appeared at the door of Harriet's bedroom, popping his head in to just check the lay of the land, so to speak, he was surprised to see her there, sorting the washing from a basket and putting it in the wardrobe. But he was even more surprised to see what she was wearing.

Lacy black knickers stretched over a very neat little backside. That was it, nothing else. Her legs were long and shapely and her bare breasts stood firm and with erect nipples, dragged his eyes to the upper part of her body. Harriet became aware of him looking at her and she turned to face him and she smiled.

"Hi Henry! Good to see you up and about. A bit worried when you didn't show up on time last night. Figured we must have scared you both. Your dear wife is still waiting for my husband to wake up, I think."

Henry stared back at this apparition.

"I suppose time is up and you are about to send me home, Harriet, what a pity."

Harriet walked across to him and took his hand.

"I'm not letting you go anywhere, Henry. At least, not until you've fucked me dear man. And I also need your help with something else that your wife tells me you are good at."

Henry was trying to take it all in but was having difficulty taking his eyes off of this beautiful creature.

"What is she suggesting, Hetty?"

Hetty reached for the top of her knickers and pushed them down over her thighs and turned her back on him and pointed to her bum.

"I want what you sometimes give to Lottie. There is lube here beside the bed. So hopefully, from a slow start, you will make me happy, Henry. But let me help you. Come and kiss my breasts you lovely man and we'll see how we get on. Maybe you should undress first, though."

Henry remembered what Lottie had told him about their neighbour. She had said that Hetty could be very analytical. Henry was seeing this now. He wasn't sure how to turn this visually ravishing creature from a seeming autonomic effigy into an emotional sexually active woman.

Henry thought things through quickly and came up with a plan.

"Sorry, Harriet. I can only make love to you in the kitchen. I'm going in search of coffee. Why dont you bring a doona for the kitchen table. See you down there."

Harriet was agog at Henry's response. How dare he not respond the way she expected him to. She fumed and threw the last of the washing into the wardrobe. Then she dragged the doona from the bed, down the stairs and into the kitchen. Henry was standing at the sink naked and when he turned and smiled, she saw his huge erection, upright, standing against his belly.

Henry walked over to the confused Harriet and put his arms around her neck and pulled her face to his and kissed her gently. He then collected the doona from the floor and spread it over the kitchen table. Then he turned Harriet and bent her over the table and removed her knickers. He pushed his face into her backside and wetted and licked her then he parted her legs and put his shaft against her vagina.

A slow determined shagging commenced. Harriet gasped but showed no other signs of emotion.

Henry picked up the bottle of olive oil from the kitchen bench and ran a trickle down between Harriet's buttocks. Then he rubbed oil on his cock and manoeuvred it so that the head just entered Harriet's tiny anus. Again, she gasped.

"If this is your first time, sweet lady, it might be uncomfortable. What I suggest is that you make regular visits to our place and together with our mutual love, Lottie, we'll explore your buttocks together. Do you agree with that proposal, Hetty?"

The magic of words! Harriet saw a plan and one she could handle and enjoy, hand-in-hand with her lady love, and she responded in the only way she could.

Harriet, gently removed Henry from her buttocks and turned and smiled lovingly at him and kissed him passionately.

"Oh yes, Henry, I would love that. And may I say that you have a beautiful cock."

Harriet rubbed her hands all over his body – his buttocks – his back – his chest and neck, and most lovingly, his cock. Then Harriet picked up his cock between her finger, and dropped to her knees and began to suck him. Then she stopped and looks up at him lovingly.

"Now fuck me my darling man, just like you fuck our beautiful Lottie. I want to feel what she feels. My pussy is yours and hers forever. Do whatever you want. Every part of me is yours."

Across the road, Charlotte is also doing housework things in the bedroom – wearing just her pyjamas – when she is suddenly face to face with her showered and refreshed neighbour. George stands in the doorway, wearing just a towel and stares at her.

"Good morning, George. Hope you slept well."

Charlotte smiled her beautiful smile. Then she turned away and bent over, making sure her silk covered derriere stood out to capture his gaze.

"Good morning, Lottie. My God, you are so sexy."

Lottie shook her bootie provocatively.

"Well that's great George but your words are not enough for my butt. It wants to feel your cock. I love cock between my buttocks, George. I'm sure my husband would have told you that."

Charlotte turned and looked at George. Then she pushed down her pyjama bottoms and turned her magnificent arse towards her neighbour.

"Please, George! Pretty please! Fuck it George! Fuck it now!"

George crossed the room in one bound and grabbed her beautiful bum and fell to his knees, kissing and licking it. Then he lifted his cock and spread her buttocks with his hands and looked at the well oiled pre-prepared hole.

"Thats a good boy, George. Now give the lady your hard-on. Now fuck it silly, George. I know you've secretly wanted to for years."

George pushed in hard and Lottie lifted her head and rolled back her eyes.

"Yes, George, that is beautiful. I love it. Just don't stop. There is no hurry.

You and I can do this all day if you wish. Your wife says I can keep you here as long as I like."

George heaved himself against Lottie's butt even harder.

"Oh yes! And George?"

"Yes?"

"Hetty asked me to tell you that she would like her tiny butt fucked too. Do the right thing by her, George. If you do, I'll come over sometimes and you can have us together and fuck both our bums."

George was panting but was happy to keep going for ever.

"Promise, Lottie?"

"Yes, George, I promise. Now I want to reach between my legs and play with your balls, George. Would you mind?"

SIX

CUCKOLDING THE CUCKOLDS

Harriet had just served coffee and Charlotte beamed at her from across the kitchen bench. It was their first get to-gether after the sharing event.

"I think it all went well, darling, apart from the boys not coming home when we expected them."

"Yes, Hetty! No complaints from me, and I've been told that we will see you at our place for a threesome sometime soon. Henry is very keen and so am I."

The two eyed each other lovingly.

"And I wouldn't be surprised to hear that your man was showing interest in that other little spot, darling. I know your a bit coy about it so maybe you won't want to tell me if it happens."

The two women laughed.

"Now I have some news, Lottie. When I was putting things in the washing machine this morning, I found a card in George's trouser pocket. I think you and I might find it of great interest."

Harriet reached down and opened a draw beside her and retrieved the card.

"I know it wasnt there when we went out to dinner. If I was a suspicious wife I'd swear this is conected to the sweet smells issuing from our blokes when we checked them yesterday morning. Have a look."

Charlotte took the card and read the information.

"Esme & Candice Longford, No.1 Longford Apartments, Wilmington Street, Woollahra. Wow! Sounds like they might own the apartment block."

"Indeed. I can just see two bored wealthy sisters looking to break the monotony of a Friday night at home and wandering down to the restuarant."

The two friends looked at each other and smiled.

"Will we, darling?"

"Yes, lets. It can't do any harm and if our inquiries lead nowhere, then it won't matter."

"And if it turns out to be who we think it might be, then what, Hetty?"

"I guess we'll just have to thank them for doing our job for us; showing our boys how to swing."

Much merriment was shared as Charlotte and Harriet joked about the possibilities.

"They might tell us what turned the boys on in the first place. Love to know how it all unfolded. I bet the ladies had to do the chatting-up. Our blokes were too enebriated to plan a move. And I wonder if they'd oblige us with a blow-by-blow picture?"

"Oh Charlotte. I love you. Maybe we'd all become friends and invite them over for caring and sharing moments."

"Or perhaps they would invite us to meet their other conquests. Goodness! It's all getting more exciting by the minute."

After an internet search and a drive-bye, Charlotte and Harriet were ready to make a phone call. They would say they were looking at moving in to the area and that a friend had given them their phone number and suggest they might be able to help.

"Hopefully, they will suggest we come in for an apartment inspection. Once we've met them, we can fess-up or string them along for a while."

It is oft said that once we think about something, it usually happens much quicker than we planned. So it was for Charlotte and Harriet.

The very well dressed lady behind the desk at the office of Longford Apartments smiled as she greeted and introduced herself to Charlotte and Harriet. But her smile changed slowly as she looked at the two.

They might not have noticed it but Ms Longford's attention became much more attentive as it dawned on her who she was looking at. Esme Longford recognised the two as being the companions of the two men she and her sister had recently entertained. She remembered watching the women put on their coats before leaving the restaurant.

"Now do I understand that you are looking to rent, or was it to purchase, an apartment in the area?"

"Well a lot depends on what we see and what we feel we can do with it. Anything you could show us now would get us started. You would appreciate that we've only just decided to look around."

Esme got up and came around from her desk to look over her prospective clients and she liked what she saw.

"Give me a moment if you would. I was about to send a short text to someone whose waiting to hear from me. I'll just go into the back office and get the details and send them. I won't be long."

As the woman disappeared, Charlotte and Harriet smiled at each other.

"Well, I would never have suspected that George would have gone for such a skinny woman, but then she is very sexy, don't you think, Lottie? And she's wearing very expensive clothes, I noticed."

Charlotte laughed. "Not sure that men take much notice of the quality of garments."

As the two laughed quietly in the front office, Esme was whispering on the phone to her sister in the apartment next door.

"They're definitely the wives, Candy. It could be fun. Are you ready? I'll bring them in."

Esme reappeared and announced that she didn't have an apartment for viewing except her own, and would that be all right and when the two women said it would be fine, Esme produced a key and led them out of the office to the door marked No.1, just a couple of steps away.

"My sister, Candice is in. We share the office job most of the time. Come in, please."

If Charlotte and Harriet were expecting someone very different, Candice was in fact a twin. Not only that, both women were dressed very much the same, the same lipstick and nail polish, their floral dresses were an identical cut; only the floral patterns were different. Both wore expensive Italian sandals on bare suntanned feet and legs.

Charlotte and Harriet arrived at the same conclusion at the same time and looked at each other and smiled. Yes! George and Henry could easily have been picked up by these two super live ladies.

Things now moved even faster.

"Candy? Meet Charlotte and Harriet who I recognise as the lovely wives of George and Henry, although I cant be sure which is whose wife."

Charlotte and Harriet were momentarily taken aback but quickly regained their poise.

"Welcome! Its good to meet you both. Forgive us if we look like we're checking you out, the truth is, we are. You're both super attractive and we really appreciate beautiful women. Tea or coffee?"

Charlotte answered quickly.

"I'd love a coffee, Candice. What about you, Harriet?

Harriet, always the least spontaneous, rallied.

"Coffee too please Candice."

"So are you both here to check us out too! And are you unhappy with us or can we just relax and enjoy coffee and cake and each other while we also check how horny we're feeling?"

Charlotte was quick to answer.

"The truth is, Esme, you helped us enormously."

"We did. Wow! We've never had a cuckolded wife say that to us before. How did we help?"

Harriet was staring at Candice's long tanned legs as she bent over the the dining table to lay out the refreshments. She thought how sexy the woman looked and tried to imagine George getting his hands on that neat little bum. Then she made herself come back to the conversation, only to notice that Esme was watching her very closely.

"Harriet and I both wanted to get our blokes into a sharing mode in preparation for a swingers party we would all attend in a week or so."

"Ursula's?"

"Yes! So you two got them started and we appreciate it. But of course, curiosity got the better of us and here we are. We hope you're not too bothered by our intrusion."

"Come and get your coffee, girls." Candy called from the dining area.

They all stood up and moved towards the table.

"Well, Candy? Are we bothered. We could say we were which would give us an excuse to punish them. That could be fun. What do you think, my caring and sharing sister?"

"Hmm! It's tricky, them barging in here like this. They must realise that we are entitled to some retribution. Yes, I think we do have to punish them, Esme. Will we take them down to the cellar and chain them to the wall and whip them?"

Charlotte and Harriet looked at each with open mouths. The deadpan face and voice of Candice was frighteningly convincing. This must be a joke, surely.

"No, no dearest sister. You're being overly dramatic as usual. My suggestion is that we demand that they let us sit on their laps and let them soothe our hurt feelings with loving kisses. But they would need to remove their dresses and skirts first."

"Oh all right Esme. I like that idea."

Charlotte and Harriet looked at each other, both with a light in their eyes.

"I suppose we'll have to do what they ask, Harriet. We have offended them."

Charlotte stood up and lifted her dress up over her head. Then Harriet stood and unzipped her skirt and dropped it to the floor.

Two excited ladies stood up and stood in front of Charlotte and Harriet. Then Candice sat on Harriet's legs and Esme sat on Charlotte's legs.

Then both women put their arms around their captive visitors and kissed them and as they did so, two sets of hands lifted the hems of their floral dresses and caressed their knees and legs.

Esme and Candice stood up and removed their dresses, and, taking each of their visitors by the hand, they led them to the a double bed in a room next door.

As the excited loving ladies explored each other, touching and slapping and pinching and palming each others special places, the forever over-thinking Harriet – but only for one moment – imagined George and Henry enjoying the sisters on this very same bed.

Then, as she and Candy swapped partners, she welcomed Esma sliding on top of her and beginning to hump her, she forgot about George.

Harriet looked across at her other love, Lottie, who was rolling on top of the newly arrived Candice. Charlotte began a strong thrusting and humping along with a passionate kissing session, only slowing down long enough to swap to move underneath so Candice could fuck her, pussy-to-pussy and very hard.

Then Esme got underneath Harriet and together with her sister lying beside her, the two parted their legs and reached them up in a V shape, their favourite position where they could see and admire their slender brown legs and feet waving in the air.

The sisters enjoyed this position when their friend Damian invited the insatiable sisters, as he called them, onto his large ocean-going yacht on Sydney harbour in the summer months.

Damian had an especially made lean-to rotating sun lounge at the stern. Sun bathers could strip completely knowing they were hidden from the eyes of people with binoculars sitting on balconies and in sunrooms in the mansions that lined the harbour.

Damian would invite half-a-dozen close friends to come aboard and enjoy food and fine wines, and relax with other guests.

Esme and Candice would lay totally naked on the huge lilo that covered the floor. With their long thin brown legs spread apart and pointing upwards and with their pussy's soaking in the warm sun, they would smile up at Damian's guests and call to them to take off their clothes and join them. Damian's friends would then avail themselves of what the ladies offered and the insatiable sisters would live up to their name.

And as the afternoon moved on, selected fellow yachtsmen who were privy to the ladies presence, would pull up alongside in their dinghy's and have a moment between the girls legs before heading back to their own boat where their wives and ladyfriends and their kids and grandkids were feasting on barbecued fish and prawns.

At the end of the day, a harbour taxi would collect Esme and Candice and take them to Steyne Park jetty, only a short walk from their apartment.

Once they were home, Esme and Candice would enjoy their giant spa bath, laughing and joking about their day in the sun.

"I really enjoyed today, darling. Who had the most, Candy? I think it might have been you?"

"Probably, Esme. It certainly feels like it. I'm going to sleep well tonight."

"Fat Aldo took a long time today so that set me back a bit, timewise. I worry about his weight. His wife should ease up on the pasta. But I would'nt be surprised if she encourage's his over-eating. She is super attractive and dresses like a model. Once Aldo has passed on, she will be so rich she'll probably head off to Europe and buy an appartment and live like so many of her friends, spending part of he time here and the rest overseas.

I dreamt once that he had a heart attack when he was on me and that the medics could'nt lift him. They simply covered the two of us with the sheet we were lying on and dragged us both off to the water ambulance. I think of it every time he visits me.

Charlotte and Harriet thanked their hosts for a lovely afternoon and said how they hoped they would see each other again.

"Maybe we'll feel you up at Ursula's party," laughed Esme.

"Maybe we'll find you first. It will be funny if we have to fight our husbands to get our hands on your bums."

Esme offered Harriet a business card. "Thanks, Esme. We've already got one but I'll take another one. Then I can put George's back in his pocket."

Esme and Candice laughed, enjoying the thought of poor George scrambling to find his card.

"Maybe I should have one, too. Just in case Hetty and I fall out and I need to console myself with someone delicious, close by!"

Again, there was much laughter. Then Esme became serious.

"Maybe we could have lunch over the road together, sometime. It would be fun to get to know each other with our clothes on."

With much hugging, the four women parted.

"Well, Hetty. I think we are fully prepared for Ursula's party where maybe we will discover more fun things about enjoying other people like we did this afternoon."

As the two walked the short distance home, Harriet put her arm around Lottie.

"I love you, Lottie."

Charlotte slipped her arm around her friends waist.

"I love you too, Hetty."

SEVEN

THE PARTY

Madison was offered employment to work at a function organised by a friend of Robyn's. This was pitched as a house party but only for grown ups. Its real purpose was not in doubt; men and women getting together. Swinging by a different name.

This was the third of Robyn's close friend Ursula's monthly get togethers and with word of what was offered spreading fast, it was now drawing in people from other genteel suburbs close by.

Madison came to the house early as suggested, and introduce herself to Ursula who welcomed her with the full up and down visual inspection. Ursula smiled her approval with what she saw.

Madison immediately saw that Ursula fitted the same mould as Robyn; a voluptuous older woman with what Madison suspected was a suspiciously similar sexual appetite.

As instructed, Madison had dressed conservatively, wearing black slacks, a white polar-necked skivvy and low heeled black shoes. Her hair was tied up in a bun.

She had been told on the phone that in no way was she to compete with the party-goers. If Maddy had dressed in the clothes that she usually wore when she strutted her stuff at parties, then she would have been seen as obvious competition to the female guests and indeed, a major distraction.

"Robyn said you were intelligent and looked good and suggested you would be the right person to be my eyes and ears and general help. From what I'm seeing, it looks as though she was right.

"I'm sure you will understand, darling, when I say that you should not tempt our visitors from either the partner they arrive with or the person they are hoping to connect with. Not that you aren't allowed to enjoy yourself. Just maybe fill your own needs later in the evening with a little something on the side although nothing that would attract too much attention."

"I have quite a lot of experience, Ursula and I can assure you that my desires are well controlled," Madison replied with a reassuring smile.

"Now I've made this pin for you Madison. I suggest you wear it to officially inform people of your status and also to help avoid unwanted advances."

Ursula leant forward and gently pinned the label on Madison's chest. It read: Madison: Information and Party Advice.

Madison bathed Ursula in her most disarming smile.

Ursula smiled back.

"Make yourself known to the head waitress. Her name is Inala and I've told her about you. I hope you enjoy yourself. If your presence tonight works for both of us, Madison, then I will be looking to employ you on a regular basis.

"Oh yes! There is one more thing you should know. I've implemented a second feature to the evenings entertainment which not many people will discover but which I think will become popular over time. I call it The Dunking Paddock and it's basically a private dogging venue situated out in the little paddock which can be reached via a gate in the back wall at the far end of the garden.

"It is free to members but will also be available as a stand alone event sometime soon. Men attending on their own will pay to enter. Women will be admitted free but for safety's sake they need to be accompanied by a male partner; a husband, brother or whatever.

"Not sure yet how it will go. You could keep an eye out and let me know what you think. Ultimately it will be up to the ladies whether or not it will work. If they like it then we'll keep it going."

Ursula smiled and suggested Madison wander about and familiarise herself with the house.

"The lights are dimmed throughout the house. There are many rooms and nooks and cranny's which you will discover.

"One last thing that I should mention. There is one very large room on the ground floor where I've taken out the wall between two bedrooms. We call this The Pink room because it is lit with a subdued pink lighting. The floor is covered in mattresses, pillows and cushions and it is the place where most find their way to eventually and where they can offer themselves to all. An open market, so to speak.

"I've given you a tiny bedroom at the top of the stairs where you can put your bag and coat or just get a moment to yourself. Here is the key. First door on the left. Oh yes. I've put a small pocket torch on the bed which you may wish to carry for emergency use. Have fun darling. I'll hopefully be very busy so any questions you have should be made to Inala and not to me."

Madison thanked Ursula and picked up her bag and headed up the wide staircase. She deposited her things on the bed in her room and thought what a great little hideaway it was. The little torch seemed like a good idea so she popped it into her pocket.

Just as she was about to leave, Madison remembered something and went back to her bag. She had bought herself a present on-line. Madison smiled and gently fondled it. She decided to wear it tonight, just to get used to the feel of having it there. A little lubricant helped and suddenly she was in charge of the new toy and thinking how big it felt but then she assumed she would soon adjust to it.

A pink ribbon belt fell out of the box and Madison stared at it, wondering what it was for. Then she looked at the instruction leaflet and smiled then wrapped the ribbon around herself and tightened it. Now she could see why it was a good idea. It held everything tight against her belly and made the new thingy practically invisible inside her panties and slacks.

Wandering about the house looking in all of the rooms and noticing the hidden alcoves was exciting. A narrow back stairway lead to what must have once been servants quarters. Doors led to tiny rooms each housing a single bed with hardly room to move.

In the fading light, she inspected the garden and even ventured into The Dunking Paddock which boasted a number of solid double bed-like wooden bases spread about, each topped with a soft straw-filled palliasse.

When she felt she had a reasonable mental picture of the property in her head, Madison went back to where she could observe the large room and main reception area, peering between the steps of the wide open staircase. Then she ventured out and found a deep arm chair to bury herself in, just near where the stairs began and alongside the entrance to the ground floor passageway.

Observing people arriving and reading their body language was most enjoyable, as was assessing people by their looks. Madison looked forward to listening in to their conversations where possible. The whole idea excited her. This was her night to be the absolute voyeur.

A few people had already been shown through to the big lounge room where drinks were being served.

One couple had seated themselves on one of the three large settees and were holding hands and looking both at each other and towards the door, watching to see others arriving.

Then a party of three arrived. Madison figured that the two largish women were probably sisters in their mid forties and the man would have been a husband of one of them or perhaps an older brother or maybe just a friend.

Big smiles on big ladies and eager looks of anticipation radiated around the room as the group moved to take a seat on a settee.

After they had sunk into the soft cushions, both women instinctively moved their hands to pull down the hems of their short skirts over their chubby legs to try to give a sense of modesty, not that it made a lot of difference. Their heavy stockinged legs and tight strappy high heels along with their exaggerated make-up signalled they were dressed for an evening of fun or hopefully, debauchery.

Madison realised that she was already loving this job. Watching people prepare for a night of sexual adventure was truly exciting.

The first couple she had noticed suddenly decided to move and rose and headed towards the settee close to Madison but as they were about to sit down, the man turned and looked towards the door and Madison heard him speak.

"They're here darling. Look! I said they'd come."

His partner stopped staring across at Madison and looked back to the main door.

"Oh yes, Arnold, they did come. I'm so pleased to see them. I just hope they remember us and are pleased to see us."

Arnold waved across the room and Madison saw a man and woman waving back and moving slowly across to join the first couple.

"Well Megan. Happy now? I know how much you enjoyed Ray."

The lovely lady's face took on the perfect blush and she looked at Arnold with a kindly knowing smile. Then, without any indication to her man, she looked quickly past him, across at the nearby Madison and beamed a beautiful smile.

"And I believe you enjoyed his lovely wife just as much, darling. I just hope they remember us as fondly. From my memory, Susannah was blown away when you took her up against the wall."

Arnold laughed.

"As I remember it, you both came at about the same time. Ray nailed you against the same wall and it all took off from there."

Madison was wildly excited by what she was hearing. On top of that, she was instantly in love with the lithe wifey Megan, staring at her in her floral dress and seamed stockings and modest heels. Madison suddenly found herself wanting to lie on top of Megan and do loving things with her beautiful and seemingly innocent body.

"Maybe those American TV shows depicting attractive bored housewives were really true to life after all?" Madison mused.

As the newly arrived couple came closer, Madison noticed certain similarities. Both women were tall and lithe and both stood a half head higher than their husbands. The men were stocky and likely quite muscular.

"Hi, Arnold and Megan. So glad you are here. Susannah was terrified you wouldn't show up. I assured her that you seemed to have as good a time as us when we first met so you were sure to be here."

Madison was now in love with all four. Susannah in a plain summer frock and stockings and heels was almost identical to the lovely Megan. And Maddy would have willingly allowed either or both of the two jolly men to pin her against a wall and do what ever they wanted.

There was an awkward moment of silence as the two couples continued smiling at each other, neither pair sure of what to say or do next. Madison noticed the excitement shining through the blushes on both womens faces and she tried to live their anticipation.

Then Susannah reached across and took Megan's hand and Madison saw Megan squeeze the other's hand signifying a common purpose. Then in a little voice, Megan spoke.

"We both liked what we did last time and would happily do it again if that is okay with you boys? And, I should ask, if you are both still okay with us gals getting it from other men later? And we so loved seeing you with other women didn't we Susannah?"

Susanna grinned. "Oh, yes! Especially towards the end when that very big lady made you both fuck her, and then suggested you both try to fuck her at the same time. Megan and I were both quietly cheering you on. It was so hot."

Arnold and Raymond exchanged glances, silently indicating that a repeat of last time was exactly what they wanted. Then each took the hand of their partner and placed it in the hand of the other man.

Madison saw the smiles widen on the faces of the two ladies as they saw that it was all about to happen and she knew exactly what they were feeling.

In fact, at that moment Madison felt the exact same excitement and noticed that the crotch of her knickers were suddenly feeling moist despite the presence of her new toy.

As the two happy couples turned towards the staircase, it was all Madison could do to not get up and follow them.

"Oh my god! This job might be too exciting. I will need to be a little more careful about how close I get to peoples fantasies."

Madison looked back to where the couples were just disappearing at the top of the stair and she thought how, in only a few moments, Arnold and Raymond will have the pants off Susannah and Megan and be happily climbing under those summer frocks and in between the girls beautiful thighs and shafting the two of them against a lucky upstairs wall. Bliss!

It was good that the four lovers had gone. Now Madison could get back to work and concentrate on what was happening in the large lounge. The big ladies had disappeared although the male member of the group was still near the sofa in conversation with two men.

Madison scolded herself for not being more observant and chastised herself severely. Then she saw the big ladies emerge from the door that led to the bathroom and walk over to the settee. The two men turned and each held out a hand then led the women away along the corridor beside the stairs, heading no doubt, to one of the many bedrooms.

Things were definitely getting busier and Madison realised that she wouldn't be able to scrutinise all of the people to the same degree that she had so far.

Couples wandered everywhere. Quite a number were women in pairs but most comprised a man and one or sometimes, two woman.

Madison saw a group of three men in their early to late thirties, checking out the women spread around the lounge. They seemed to be targeting women on their own or women in pairs or at least those without a male partner. The men would approach a woman and after a few moments Madison would see a woman nodding her head indicating a negative response and the men would move away. They were seemingly being knocked back by every woman they approached and Madison tried to guess what the men were proposing.

As Madison scanned the crowd, she noticed that the three men were heading towards a tiny woman who had caught Madison's attention earlier. It wasn't just her diminutive size that was interesting. The woman was dressed in a most sexually provocative manner, much more sexually overt than anyone else in the room. She wore a low cut red top and a very short and tight red miniskirt. Her shapely legs were sheathed in white stay-up stockings topped with frills and her strappy red sandals could not have had higher heels.

There was something else about this little lady. She seemed very active, or was she agitated? She stood up and sat down constantly and fiddled with the hem of her short mini skirt and sometimes lifted a leg and removed a high stiletto shoe and inspected it and then immediately refitted it to her tiny foot.

Madison wondered if the woman was okay. Maybe she was exhibiting signs of the influence of medication or another substance of some kind? Madison couldn't be sure.

Just as Madison thought she should wander over and see if help was needed, the three men approached and began a conversation with the tiny sexy looking woman. It was only moments before Madison saw the woman nodding in agreement. Then she took hold of two of the mens hands and let them lead her down the passage beside the stairs.

Madison knew enough to guess what was being offered by the men and she wondered if the little lady had any inkling of what she was in for. If she didn't then her first gang bang was likely to be a shock but Madison reasoned that maybe this was what the woman was desperately wanting; and who was Madison to assume otherwise or pass judgement. At least there was a modicum of care in selecting who was admitted to this event and hopefully there would be a level of civility among the three men so that their sexual encounter would be satisfying to all parties. Madison prayed that this would be so.

Things were moving faster. Not only that, a number of the increasingly large throng now overflowing the lounge were showing early signs of losing their inhibitions as a result of simply drinking a glass or two of Champagne or simply being carried along with the euphoria of anticipation. This was manifesting itself in a sudden increase in touching and feeling of bodies by both sexes.

Respectable looking women had hands pressed up against the bulging fronts of mens trousers even as they remained holding hands with the man they had arrived with. One woman had already unzipped her suitor and was gently massaging his potent looking hard-on.

More often than not, the man whose crotch a woman had her hand on, had a hand not just on the woman's backsides but even under her skirt or dress, inadvertently displaying an elegant silk clad leg or even the woman's skimpy-panty clad backside and which she might wriggle provocatively in anticipation.

Madison watched as two such women smiled as each handed their partner over to the other. Then the newly connected couples smiled and then one lead the way towards the stairway, followed by the other other two, hands gently groping each other as they went.

Across the room, more people were arriving.

Of interest was the older Japanese man accompanied by three younger women. Two of the women could easily have been sisters and looked to be of Caribbean extraction. They looked extraordinarily beautiful from where Madison was sitting.

The third woman looked to be part Japanese and was also stunningly attractive in a different sort of way. She was petite and her cropped spiked orange and green hair made her the centre of attention, in particular the attention of many of the women in the room.

More people were partnering and setting off to discover secluded spots in the house where they could give vent to their lust.

Twice, Madison watched as an older woman was led away by two younger men. She also noticed a well built swarthy man with a shiny bald head being led away by two women who acted both nervously and excitedly. They kissed every few moments, maybe to reassure each other on their choice of action. Each took turns in grasping the sizeable bulge in the man's trousers even while their faces showed red with embarrassment. Tales of the potency of bald men were obviously alive and well.

Madison couldn't resist exploring her voyeur instincts more thoroughly and decided to follow the crowd even though she was the only one without a partner. She began by taking a stroll along the dimly lit passageway and discovered that what some folk were doing could be both funny or erotic or both.

"Is that you Henry? I've left my glasses in my bag and you know I'm lost without them when I'm in a dark space. It doesn't feel like you but whoever it is, it does feel nice. If you're not Henry, perhaps you should tell me your name if you are intending to get intimate with me. Even if I cannot see you properly at least I'll know who I was with. And while I'm thinking about it, where are we going?"

There was silence, then a woman's voice close by answered.

"I think you've got my George, Lottie, and I'm pretty sure that what I've got in my hand belongs to your Henry. Is it okay if he knobs me darling? George will give you a good go, I'm sure. A couple of drinks and he usually wants it doggy style. And he'll go forever. Just thought you should know. I'm sure you will love it.

"Oh, and I think we're heading for the Pink Room, Lottie."

There was silence for a moment as Charlotte reviewed her situation.

"Well, Hetty. If we both enjoy today, I suppose it could be something we can do at home. Would you be up for it? Swapping our husbands on a Sunday afternoon could become something we could do instead of going for a drive."

"Indeed, Lottie! Being knobbed sounds much better than going to a plant nursery or art gallery. And if it works, we could ask our neighbours Doreen and Stacey if they were interested in doing it. I reckon both of their blokes could be good for something a little different.

Madison couldn't stop herself giggling and thought how this must be the best paid job in the whole world. Then she heard voices coming from a bedroom and stopped and peeped inside.

"For goodness sake, if you're brothers then surely you must know who usually goes first?"

A well built attractive older woman had stripped down to just her stockings and shoes and was sitting back on the bed with her legs wide apart and her curly-haired vulva on full display. Her large solid breasts stood out provocatively and she held a solid cock in each hand.

Madison had noticed the woman earlier and watched as the hands of the two men, most likely in their late twenties, were offered by another older woman. After the three headed off down the passageway the woman who handed them over stared after them then took out a handkerchief and dabbed her eyes.

"No, please stop it? We're not going to do the eeny-meeny miny-moe thing again. I've caught my tigers by their cocks so just give it me. However much you holler, I'm not letting either of you go. One of you just fuck me. Now! Or is there something else going on?

"Okay! Now I've obviously missed something."

The woman sat back and thought for a while, then she leant over and whispered in one man's ear, and then she immediately did the same with the other one.

There was a sudden flurry of activity and the lady on the bed was suddenly rolled onto her knees with her bum in the air and vocalising her excitement. Between screams she managed to whisper, "Christ! So that's how she did it?"

Madison closed the door quietly, still giggling and set out along the passageway. Surely someone somewhere must be just lustfully doing it, she thought.

When Madison neared the bend in the passageway she at last heard the plaintive tones of a "Yes, Yes, Yes! Harder you beautiful bastard," and she thought the world was at last working the way it should. She gently pushed open a door and peered into the gloom.

The two big ladies she had watched leave with two men earlier were on their knees on a big bed, heaving their bodies every which way. Their buttocks slapped in noisey unison as the two strong males shoved energetically into their pussies.

"Have you bitches had enough yet?" said one of the men, quietly.

"Or are your wet cunts ready for another round?" echoed the other man.

Madison heard the women sobbing and wailing and wondered if they were okay. Then a cracked voice called out.

"Give us some more cock. Just get on with it."

The two men pulled out and swapped places then reinserted themselves in the wet hairy places being so generously offered.

"Okay Spike. Lets go!"

The women screamed and began thrusting their rear ends back up to meet their pleasure providers.

"Yes, Yes, Yes!"

Again, Madison backed out of the room quietly.

Time had moved on. People all over the house were doing it as Madison wandered happily along the passage until she came to the door marked The Pink Room. She could hear a low hum of voices and sounds. At first she thought it better that she not go in incase she was seen as another person of interest. But then she thought again and decided that she probably needed to see what was going on simply to get on-the-job experience about something she had not yet seen.

Madison went in and found a spot to hide beside the coat and dress racks behind the door.

Maddy saw that this is were it all really happens late in the day, The Grand Finale. If a girl hadn't had enough elsewhere, here is where she should end the evening.

There were at least forty bodies spread across the room and across each other. Legs and backsides waved in the air and there was an enormous amount of thrusting going on.

Madison noticed that there were many woman embracing and kissing and touching each other. Whether they were on their hands and knees being fucked doggy style by enthusiastic males or on their backs getting a standard shafting, at least half the ladies had a hand exploring the woman laying next to her. It was then that Madison spotted Megan and Susannah. They were side by side and both were on their knees each getting a slow doggy shagging by keen and determined males.

Meagan's face was almost touching the naked rear of the woman in front of her.

On either side of them, women – who were also receiving an energetic workout from a man – reached out to fondle the breasts of Madison's two favourite housewives.

Madison looked around the floor in search of Arnold and Raymond and eventually she discovered them at opposite ends of the room, each with a woman sitting on them, energetically rising up and down on their cocks and seemingly mouthing words or sounds that Madison could not decipher above the noise.

Both men seemed happy with their situations and they were obviously happy in the knowledge that their wives on the other side of the room were getting well and truly poked.

Madison was about to leave when she recognised a voice. The woman in front of Meagan was humping another woman.

The women underneath her was gasping and writhing under the energetic attention she was enjoying.

"How come you haven't done it to me this way before, Harriet?"

"Never thought about it until I saw those two women over there doing it. I'm loving it Lottie. I hope you are. Give me your hand. I want it on my tits."

Madison looked around and noted that indeed, there were a number of women atop other women. In some instances they were part of a threesome being recipients of male attention from the rear.

"I'm loving it Harriet. Maybe we should do this at each others after morning tea on a Wednesday when the boys are at golf?"

"Yes, I think I'm going to want it more often, Lottie so look out. We've got a lot of catching up to do."

As Harriet rubbed herself vigorously on Lottie's large pubic mound, she felt a hand on her backside. Looking up and to the back, she observed a beautiful woman smiling at her. Then the woman spoke, quietly mouthing her words "That is so beautiful. I'd love to be your friend. I'm Megan."

Harriet slowed down and stared at Megan.

"Why not! I'm Harriet Jones. I'm the only one listed. Call me, Megan. I'd love to meet up with you."

Madison headed back along the shadowy corridor to return to her watching station.

Women on their knees on the carpet were sucking a host of cocks as well as breasts and pussies while others leant against the walls of the passage with their legs apart, their knickers down and their knees bent. Men thrusted at them and yelled and women screamed.

Happiness reigned and out in the lounge room, a couple of women who had been enjoying themselves in the Pink Room and now thought they were finished for the day, were now smiling contentedly.

But they were astonished to find themselves the centre of attention. Suddenly both were being bent over the backs of armchairs, and their dresses dragged up over their backsides by men who had happily discovered that they still had shots in their armoury and could offer a final ravishing.

On seeing what was happening, other men were suddenly discovering that they too, had something left and began to line up for a turn. But then two more women arrived from upstairs, and seeing what was going on, made themselves available by draping themselves over a settee to avail themselves of the revived cock line-up.

Only moments after she returned to stand close by her comfy chair, now home to a trouser-less man and two disheveled cock-licking ladies, Madison's world changed dramatically.

Suddenly an arm encircled Madison's waist then a small hand slid up under her skivvy and her little bra, grasping her girly breast while another arm put her neck in a stranglehold.

"I know what you need lovely lady and I'm the only person who can give it to you. Is it to be here on the carpet or do you have a preferred place? Answer me quickly you skinny bitch."

Madison smelt a rare perfume and the elegant voice of a woman was mesmerising. She was immediately in love with her assailant.

"The alcove just behind the stairs," Madison gurgled despite the choking hold around her throat.

In just moments Madison was on her back in a darkened spot which the passing crowed seemed never to notice. Hands were removing her clothing and suddenly she was in just her little red bra and matching hold ups.

"I knew it. I can spot one from across the room. But you won't have this for long darling or at least not until I've finished with you.

Madison's new strapless dildo stood up, waving its head, happy to be released from her knickers and the pink restraining strap.

Above her loomed the beautiful lesbian with the orange and green spiked hair and Madison could see that the woman was wearing a rubber cock like her own and she knew that she was about to be fucked with it.

Madison's body screamed with excitement. This is what she really, really wanted. Life had been leading her towards this moment. A full lesbian showdown – woman to woman and no men allowed.

"What will I call you?" Madison gasped.

"Sara! And you?"

"Madison!"

Sara fondled Madison between the legs and gently removed her strapless toy. Then without further talk or action, Sara inserted her rubber cock into Madison and began a rigorous dance of love that Madison would never forget.

"Oh Sara! Yes! Yes!"

Madison looked up into the eyes of her new magic mistress and smiled with glazed eyes, heaving herself upward every once in a while as Sara moved backward and forward to a different tune. Sara's eyes were often closed and her small smiling mouth would pout and sometimes she would moan in her obvious ecstasy.

EIGHT
WHAT A GIRL REALLY NEEDS

Madison didn't know how long the two woman had been standing watching her and Sara make love, but when she heard one of them speak she thought she'd gone to heaven.

"Now that is what a girl really needs, Susannah."

Megan and her friend were enthralled and both women watched with their hands up under their skirts.

Madison moved her head and looked up at the two gorgeous women, then before she could stop herself, she smiled her most loving smile and patted the carpet on either side of her and her lover, gesturing to them to lie down beside them, and without a moments hesitation, the two slid down and laid back on the carpet and stared closely at the beautiful lovemaking scene before them.

When Sara became aware that she had an audience, she stopped what she was doing and looked at each of them. Then, in that beautiful Kentish private school voice she spoke.

"Please make yourselves comfortable ladies and don't go away. My name is Sara. You will be next; and you can touch us if you wish."

Then she buried the multi-coloured rubber cock deep in Madison's vulva and Madison screamed and orgasmed.

Sara removed herself and gently returned Madison's dildo to her, placing it back in what was now a well lubricated vagina. Then she moved over and lowered herself between the legs of a stupefied Susannah who squealed and spoke gibberish as she excitedly reached forward with both hands to take hold of Sara's rubber gift and pull it towards her crotch.

"Now, you straight slutty house wife. You will never forget the moment when I made you see that you should give yourself to a women."

"I'm going to make you appreciate true pussy power. You want that don't you, you sexy little tart? Cunts as well as cocks will be your future and you will thank me for that."

Sara pushed into the more than ready randy woman beneath her and Susannah let out a piercing scream and began to gasp loudly and call out.

"Yes, oh yes, Sara. Show me the way; I want it! I want it!"

Then Sara leant forward and engulfed Susannah's mouth and sucked out her tongue.

Now it was Madison's and Megan's turn.

"I fell in love with you the moment I saw you sitting in the arm chair, Madison."

Megan put out her hand and touched Madison's face and then leant forward and kissed her on the lips and moments later they were fully immersed in a kissing frenzy.

"I wanted you too. You are so beautiful. I want you so much and I will keep wanting you."

The two women hugged each other, kissing and sighing as they did so.

"You can shag me with that thing if you want to, Madison," Megan whispered. "Whatever you want my darling. I just want you every which way, and very likely I will want you in my life forever."

Madison gently slid herself on top of Megan and their hands felt each other in excited anticipation and they both sighed and groaned with the intense feelings they were experiencing.

With their lips pressed hard together, Madison parted Megan's legs and rested the end of her rubber cock against her neat lightly haired and extremely wet vagina.

"Oh Megan! I give you this with my love."

Madison gently pushed into Megan whose vagina seemed to just open and swallow her rubber offering and suddenly their bodies were gently moving together in a dance of passion.

"Oh my God! Oh yes! Please Madison. I love you! I will want much more of this."

There came a moment when all four women paused and reviewed their situations. Then Sara spoke.

"The only way a woman can free herself from the restrictive male dominated ethos is to enjoy making love to women as well as to men.

"Now go forth and seduce your friends and neighbours, young and old. Let female love lead the way and free you from disappointment. You will never regret it."

Sara dressed and put her clothes in order, hiding her male appendage beneath her elasticised knickers. She smiled at everyone and murmured a "thank you" then headed off across the room towards her companions.

Susannah rolled over and smiled at Megan and Madison.

"Can I have a little bit of your friend, Megan? Right now I just want to be fucked by a woman for ever. Pretty please? And we must get ourselves a couple of these rubber doodads. We are definitely going to need them from now on."

Megan smiled down at Madison and took hold of her rubber cock and rubbed it.

"Could you give my friend a little a bit of this my love? I can see that like me, she is going to want a lot of it in the future."

Madison smiled up at her new love. Then she rolled over and pushed Susannah back down on the carpet and slowly shagged the woman who groaned and called out while Megan lightly fingered Madison's buttocks and breasts and kissed her shoulders and her neck and her back and whispered, "Yes! Yes, fuck the lovely bitch, my darling. Then give it to me again. I love you."

But Madison was forced to stop and she looked at the two women and said how she should be getting back to work or she might get the sack. They all laughed and kissed and Megan gave Madison her telephone number and made her promise to call.

———

Back at her watching station beside the arm chair, Madison saw that everyone had indeed moved on. Disheveled people who had obviously finished their escapades were appearing from the passageway and others staggered down the stairs. They milled around the room looking at each other seemingly in no hurry to leave.

A couple of women seemed to have mislaid their dresses, adorning the room in just their underwear and shoes, casually signalling their satisfaction with the happy sensual experiences they had recently enjoyed. Many wore dreamy smiles while others looked dazed, even shocked.

Most seemed oblivious to her, but then Madison felt a hand on her backside. The tiny woman who had gone off with the three men was standing and looking at Madison. She beamed up at her, reading her name tag, and in a tiny low voice, announced that her name was Veronica and she needed a woman to finish her off and she had worked out that Madison would be the best person to help her.

Looking at the tiny sexy apparition beside her and trying to focus on the woman's request was at first a shock. But then, still hot from her most recent adventure, Madison smiled and mumbled "Sure! Love to! Follow me, Veronica." Taking the woman by the hand, Madison led her up the stairs to her room.

The tiny Veronica melted under Madison's wanton lesbian advances, taking delight in screaming and thrusting her lovely body every which way. Madison was giving Veronica exactly what she wanted and what Madison wanted too. Veronica gurgled and moaned and called out for more and her legs pointed to the ceiling and waved as Madison worked her magic with the rubber dildo. But that wasn't all. Madison was so excited by Veronica that she wanted to eat her and biting the woman and yelling at her that she was a gang-banging slut, fuelled both womens deepest desires.

"Oh yes, Madison, I'm a gang-banging slut. Punish me you darling woman."

When Veronica came, Madison feared she had done the doll-like creature an injury. A plaintive wail issued from Veronica's lips and she shook constantly for what seemed like forever, then she was still. Madison stared down at a seemingly lifeless body.

Then Veronica's eyes opened and she smiled a beautiful smile and reached up to pull Madison's head down to be kissed.

"Save the best till last, I always say. Can I give you my telephone number Madison? You know how to give a girl what she really needs"

Madison laughed and rolled off.

"I must get back to work, Veronica. And yes, give me your number and I will give you mine. We will fuck again. You are a delight."

Madison saw that the crowd had thinned and it seemed that people were leaving in a very happy state of mind. Then she remembered being asked to check on the activities in the little paddock out the back. The Dunking area as Ursula referred to it and she quickly made her way out the back and through the garden area.

As she approached the paddock she could hear sounds through the gate so she knew that something was happening.

Madison had experienced real dogging. Madison had twice been privileged to be a part of a select dogging group, once in Sydney and also a similar event in the disused churchyard near Goulburn. Both were classic dogging situations involving vehicles, but with the benefit of exclusive membership. No smelly pervy types allowed.

The Dunking was different. There were no vehicles' from where a women could take shelter or tease the many men lining up at the car window, exposing themselves and looking forward to the woman in the car lowering the window so that she could take a lucky cock in her hand. Or if the men were really lucky, she might open the door and offer herself, and from there, she might be led or carried out onto the grass to be properly ravished.

Madison found herself reminiscing and increased her pace to more quickly discover what was happening behind the wall.

Participation at The Dunking was greater than Madison expected it would be. Most of the beds were in use plus some people were laying directly on the grass or on blankets.

The two big ladies had moved in, sharing a mattress and sharing the line-up of stiff cocks. They no longer had any clothes on except shoes and they were excitedly flaunting their enormous and insatiable rear ends to the line-up of cock-wagging males awaiting their turn. And Madison could just make out that it wasn't the usual love hole that was being filled.

Madison could have stopped and stood and watched the anal attacks but there was so much more to look at.

Wherever Madison looked, a line of men stood waiting their turn to place their cock in a woman. In some cases they stood in a circle around a woman who selected them randomly to suck. It was then that she realised that this wasn't dogging as she knew it but rather a huge gang-bang. Fun it might well be, but it lacked the excitement potential of proper dogging.

Women need to be in control and also enjoy the anticipation of not knowing what might happen next. The Dunking was all too blatantly predictable. It might work for someone once, but less so the next time.

Wandering quietly among the participants, trying not to attract male attention, Madison could see that for a number of women, this was a totally new experience and they seemed to be enjoying the novelty of it.

Her eyes were drawn to two women who were kneeling on a blanket with a row of men standing in line behind them.

As she drew closer, she realised that she had seen the women earlier and had overheard parts of their conversation.

It appears that they were next-door neighbours and both recently divorced and totally loving their new found freedom. That freedom had also involved them becoming lovers so that when Madison first saw them, they were holding hands and enthusiastically talking to two other women who were also holding hands.

"Oh we like to have men too, but since we became single and got together, life has changed. We are never lonely. And if we need a cock, we just drag in one of our neighbours who are always willing to give it to us. Their wives know about us and their husbands, and they are happy for all of us. And it gives them time to themselves to do what they want to do, be it to make love to someone elses husband or their girlfriends. Win, win all around, we think."

Madison mused that what the two were getting now would no doubt serve them well for quite some time. She also couldn't help thinking that they would need a good 'finishing off' later; but then they had each other for that.

It was late in the evening when Madison's boss appeared. Ursula looked immaculate and without any sign that she had been a party to an adventure of any sort.

"Hello Jess. I managed to take a shower and change. Always worth freshening up after a busy night.

"How has it been, darling? Everyone seemed happy as they left and all reports point to a successful outcome for all. Is that how you see it Madison? Would you say that everyone left with a happy look on their faces?"

Madison smiled back, watching Ursula relax and unfurl as she ended her day.

"From what I observed, everyone went with a happy-ever-after look on their face. Couldn't have been better, really. And I thoroughly enjoyed myself, Ursula."

Ursula looked long and hard at Madison.

"And were you able to fit in a moment of pleasure for yourself, darling?"

Madison found herself unexpectedly colouring up.

"Yes I did, Ursula. All in the line of duty really, I suppose you'd say.

Pleasant surprises often. And I really enjoyed watching and listening to people. The voyeur in me was totally stimulated and satisfied."

Ursula laughed and continued to stare at Madison.

"Was there a high point that a girl might mention?"

Madison coloured up again.

"It wouldn't be proper to talk about the clients, surely? But I fell in love at least twice and then one amazing lady with spiky green and orange hair had her way with me before I could do a thing to stop her."

Ursula leant back and laughed out loud.

"That was Sara. I sent her to you. Thought you would enjoy something a little different; and from an expert, too. The four in her party are visiting from England and all are exceptionally talented people."

Madison stared back at her boss.

"Well, that is good to know. Having such a caring sharing boss is very rare. Thank you Ursula."

Ursula reached out and took Madison's hand and drew her close, and fixed her with her beautiful smile.

"Let me kiss you Maddy. Maybe one day we will have time to play girly games together. Would you like that?"

Madison leant towards her boss and puckered up to enjoy the warmth of those large lipsticked lips and in a little voice whispered, "I would like that very much, Ursula."

NINE

EROS CRESCENT IN LOCKDOWN

EROS CRESCENT

These vignette's relate to characters from our well-known erotic trilogy. They were written following the Covid 19 lockdown. You will find a reference to the titles on our Richard Lee Publishing pages.

No one on Eros Crescent remembers exactly the moment when the words COVID-19 or Corona virus were first uttered in their houses. Needless to say, it would first have been heard on a television report and the importance of the message would have taken a few days to sink in.

The world suddenly changed. Words and phrases like lockdown and self-isolation and social distancing were suddenly in the forefront of all conversations as people enacted the requests of government and the nation to act responsibly to assist in the national objective to achieve what quickly became known as flattening the curve.

For Roger, life couldn't have been less affected. His daily routines required only that he rose from his bed, showered and shaved, ate his breakfast, went for a walk, and made sure he had sufficient pens and paper. Although it did impinge on his new paying project.

He had been asked by Desley to write another booklet similar to the one he'd written for The Club, only this was to be for The Dunking, a venue he had not yet visited or, until now, even heard of.

When Desley explained the concept and related what the setting inside the warehouse was like, Roger was very keen to get started. But the arrival of the virus put an end to that project, at least until further notice.

For Caroline and Jackie and Miranda, staying at home was what they enjoyed anyway, that is when they weren't travelling abroad or window shopping or having coffee in cafe's.

All three women managed to get back to Australia before the big lock-down. Each had worked in executive positions in London, but moving overseas brought that era to a close, although they had been invited to join similar companies in Australia.

A top of the range coffee making machine was promptly ordered along with a supply of fair trade East Timorese Maubisse, medium blend. Browsing online shops became the new window shopping.

Instagram took on a new importance as the pandemic took hold around the world. Stories and pictures of people in isolation doing amazing and sometime ridiculous things became the rage. Jackie uploaded hundreds of images of the inside and outside of the house, earning the praise of interior designers and architects.

Helen and her husband Frederico were effected in so far as Freddy's job as a flight controller at the airport was soon to be reduced in the number of hours he worked. However, there was no threat to his income as he was on standby as an essential service. But Helen's work as a freelance Human Resources consultant to industry came to a sudden halt. She embraced online conferencing on Zoom but this was no substitute for real hands-on consulting.

Helen was also restricted in her love life, already reduced as a result of her husbands responsibilities to her two lovers who had inadvertently become pregnant to him.

Sophie and Freya now spent a night a fortnight with Freddy.

Unable to visit or have visits from her own lovers, Polly or Celia Ashbee, Helen would just have to manage with her next-door neighbour, Mary. And what had looked like the answer to a maiden's prayer – The Club – was now the victim of a Covid close-down.

Mary's only loss of employment was her volunteer job at the Salvation Army Opportunity Shop which she would miss very much. She would also miss her sensual workout with her close friend Janice. But most of all, she would miss her newly found excitement at The Club which she had only recently discovered.

Her niece and housemate, Sophie, worked at a horse stud and accepted reduced hours and looked forward to doing baby things at home. Because she and Mary lived next door to Helen and Freddy, the two households would have access to each other when needed. And of course, Freddy was to be the father of Sophie's as yet unborn child.

Alice and Frey both lamented the loss of work in their jobs as school counsellors. They both loved their jobs. Both were pregnant and accepted they would be forced to spend more time at home together.

Like most of the others, they had their favourite sex toys for when they weren't knitting baby clothes or doing jigsaw puzzles. And like so many women in lockdown, they visited female friendly porn sites online. The two decided that they would always share these internet session and happily parked themselves on the sofa, transmitting the websites from their phones to the giant television set via a magic little box. This meant that the images were so big that they felt they were in the same room and this proved most enjoyable on many occasions.

Bertie and Rosa were the older folk who were most vulnerable to the virus. They were happy to be isolated although Bertie complained that he would miss his fortnightly get together for coffee and cake with Freddy and Roger.

Bertie complained that he still had much to say on the subject of breaking down the worlds dependance on the "couples model" as he called it.

"Nothing good will happen while we maintain this ridiculous habit of pairing off for life. Firstly, in over half the cases, it doesn't work and people separated or divorced.

"Secondly, it was obvious that people who stayed in these relationships were deeply frustrated by the repressive demands on them of constantly answering to another person.

"Thirdly, paternity and property ownership where the only reasons this system was maintained and with the likely end of democracy as we know it looming, house prices and pension funds and equity investments were likely to collapse.

"And I haven't even mentioned the problems of religion and religious wars."

Rosa looked at him. She loved him dearly but managed always to call him out.

"You haven't mentioned love once."

"Sex and love are two seperate things, my dear. We both know that."

Most of the close friends and relatives knew that Rosa and Bertie had broken up many years ago and taken lovers. Rosa entered relationships with her close girl friends and occasionally, a man.

Sometime later, she and Bertie got back together as a couple, but both maintained their freedom to embark on other relationships if they so chose, and this arrangement worked very well. It wasn't that they were desperate to take on other romantic adventures, but just knowing that they were free to do so, made the difference. They broke up after almost twenty years and had now been together for nearly fifty years.

"It was a necessary pause," agreed the two of them, lovingly.

It was Desley who had the most to lose but she wasn't particularly put out. The Club had to close only two short months after opening and only a few weeks after Desley had formed a partnership with her friend Sally who had opened The Dunking venue. The Dunking was closed too.

Desley welcomed the opportunity to take a rest and review everything about the club and the new venture and be ready to make any necessary changes or recommendations to Sally when they eventually reopened.

She and her partner Alvie, lived on the premises. Alvie knew about Desley's dalliances with Roger who she said she also had a soft spot for.

Desley had laughed, saying that now that they had so much time on their hands, she would endeavour to entice Roger to pop in for a threesome if Alvie didn't mind sharing. To which Alvie replied that she wanted first go.

Maria and her daughter Serina were at first, forced to stay home with grandfather Aldo and the boarder, Giorgio. They mostly worked for older people as cooks and housekeepers in the stately home of Vaucluse and Woollahra.

They successfully applied for positions with the council as carers so that they could continue working.

They both had each other and the two live-in men to play with when they felt like it plus a range of toys they enjoyed.

Maud, the owner of the music school and owner of the property at nineteen Eros Crescent found isolation difficult, severely limiting her adventures although she had managed to entertain herself with young Ashton and Damian after the two became suddenly sexually aware after falling prey to pizza nights with Edith.

And Sylvia and Stella, the two twenty-something country girl who she had enjoyed briefly when they stayed over on the night of her house warming party, seducing Maude with the help of their bunny party outfits, had booked in for music classes and accomodation just weeks before lockdown. Maud reasoned that a restricted lifestyle might not be too bad after all.

Life on Eros Crescent went on. The residents continued to love each other in many different ways and despite the sudden disruption of the pandemic, there was a feeling of optimism in the air.

Babies were on the way and new life called out for new ideas. And new ideas about how society worked were desperately needed.

Cross your sanitised fingers everyone, and hope.

TEN

RICHARD LEE PUBLISHING

Erotic Fiction

The Eros Crescent trilogy as paperbacks or ebooks:

The Fifi Code
ISBN - 978-0-909431-02-0

Eros Crescent
ISBN - 978-0-909431-05-1

Mount Eros
ISBN - 978-0-909431-08-2

Excerpts from the Eros Crescent series as paperbacks or ebooks:

Janice: A sexual enigma
ISBN - 978-0-909431-10-5
Jessica: A young woman's journey
ISBN - 978-0-909431-13-6
Helen: Enough is not enough
ISBN - 978-0-909431-14-3
Maria: Always available
ISBN - 978-0-909431-15-0
Mary: Catching up
ISBN - 978-0-909431-11-2
The Club: Ladies love it!
ISBN - 978-0-909431-11-2
Happy Honeypots: Swinging in Harmony
ISBN - 978-0-909431-20-4

Literary Fiction

Australian Short Stories

ISBN - 978-0-909431-00-6

Restless: A novel about two young men growing up

in Australia between 1900 and 1936 (Publication date not set.)

Memoir

The Kite Makers: Six years of a child's war - Britain 1939-1945 Anita Sinclair.

ISBN - 978-0-909431-16-7

Reference

Ducks for Starters: A Practical Guide to

Backyard Duck Keeping by Bruce Wicking

ISBN - 978-0-909431-18-1

Out of Print Titles

Mathematics for Young Children by Helen Western

ISBN - 978-0-909431-01-3

Currajong: For Those Whom Schools Have Failed

by Bruce Wicking

ISBN - 978-0-909431-03-7

The Puppetry Handbook by Anita Sinclair

ISBN - 978-0-909431-04-4

Wordswork by Chris Davidson & Bruce Wicking

ISBN - 978-0-909431-06-8

Sheep Production by Murray Elliott

ISBN - 978-0-909431-07-5

Sweethearts by Colin Talbot - *ISBN - 978-1-875207-02-2*

CONTACT

Publisher or review enquiries should include your full name and details in all correspondence.

Email:
countrynotebook@gmail.com